NO WAY OUT

MAFIA ELITE, BOOK 1

AMY MCKINLEY

ARROWSCOPE PRESS, LLC

No Way Out

(p) **ISBN-13**: 978-1-951919-10-8

(e) **ISBN-13**: 978-1-951919-09-2

Publisher: Arrowscope Press, LLC; www.arrowscopepress.com

Editing— Kate B., Line Editor, Brittany M., Proofreader, Red Adept Editing

Cover Design—T.E. Black Designs; www.teblackdesigns.com

Author photo provided by—Brookelyn Anhalt of lovely.life.photography; https://www.facebook.com/LovelyLifePhotography-102253596490708

Interior Formatting & Design— Arrowscope Press, LLC; www.arrowscopepress.com

THE FAMILY

Chicago Outfit
Italian-American Mafia

Caruso Family

Antonio – (father, boss)
Maria (first wife, deceased, Max's Mom)
Nicole (second wife, Tony's Mom, Elena's adopted Mom)
Tony (son)
Maximus "Max" (son)
Elena (adopted daughter)
Vito (advisor to boss)
Maria's family from Italy
Salvio "Sal" (cousin)
Cristiano (cousin)
Tommasso (cousin)
Aunt Rosa (lives in Sicily)

Brambilla Family

Benito (boss)
Julia (wife, deceased)
Liliana "Lil" (daughter)
Leonardo (underboss, cousin)
Dino (advisor to boss)
Eva (cousin)
Vincenzo (Julia's father)

La Rosa Family

Robert (boss)
Angela (wife)
Marco (son, underboss)
Nico (son)
Trey (son)
Sofia (daughter)
Maso (boss's brother, advisor)
Tom (captain)

Vitale Family

Emilio (boss)
Alessia (wife)
Enzo (son, underboss)
Emiliana "Em" (daughter)
Aldo (advisor to boss)
Renato "Ren" (captain)

Rossi Family

Frank (father, boss)
Carla (mother, deceased)
Alfonso (son, deceased)
Stefano (son, underboss – second in command)

Camila (daughter, assumed dead)
Marissa (daughter, deceased)
Drago (advisor to the boss)

Russian Mafia

Pavlov Bratva

Yuri (boss)
Mischa (wife)
Ivan (eldest son, underboss)
Victor "Vic" (son)
Katya (angel of death, assassin)

CHAPTER ONE

MAX

It's time they realize they're no longer in charge.

I folded back into the nighttime shadows of a nearby building not far from Benito Brambilla's lakefront warehouse. The shipment of drugs had arrived not long before. Heat infused my blood, despite the unseasonably cool May temperatures. The hypnotic crash of Lake Michigan's waves would soon aid our approach as we converged on our target. The wind whipped off the tumultuous water, rushing over the beach and through dark city streets. Dense cloud cover blocked the moon's rays.

A storm was coming, and not only the one nature provided.

My team—*my cousins*—were in place. Like a well-oiled machine, we would strike when the time was right. *It won't be long.*

I'd waited to enact my plan for more years than I wanted to admit. While in Sicily, we'd studied Chicago until we were as familiar with the city's grid as we were with our home in Italy. Then we examined Brambilla's holdings and how he conducted business. His father-in-law, Vincenzo, had been instrumental with that intel. Drugs, after all, were what he considered bad business, and he demanded that any involvement with them and the Brambilla line come to a swift end. I agreed. But that wasn't the only thing Vincenzo and I had discussed.

He'd given me an eight-by-ten photo of his gorgeous granddaughter, which was never far from my mind. The picture had been taken close to six months before, when she'd been on winter break from her last year of college, leaning against a window and looking out as if lost. Vincenzo had had no contact with her after her mother had been murdered—that was something we had in common. Hers was killed close to the same age as mine, leaving us both with fathers that didn't want us. Mine had abandoned me. In a way, hers had too.

Part of me worried that when I met her, I would want to kill her for taking part in the pain she and Benito had inflicted on Vincenzo. But I'd promised Vincenzo that I would keep an open mind, especially when he'd told me our situations, at heart anyway, were not that different.

From Vincenzo, I knew that Julia, his daughter, had visited him in Sicily several times with her young daughter, Liliana, before she was murdered. He had been devastated, and rightly so.

When he'd emerged from his grief and contacted Benito to arrange for a visit with his granddaughter, Benito had made threats to her safety should Vincenzo attempt to contact her—why, we weren't sure. But the end result was that Benito had poisoned his daughter's mind against her grandfather, telling her that Vincenzo was the one who'd sent men to kill her and her mother.

That was where I came in. Vincenzo wanted me to give Liliana the protection of my name, freeing her from Benito's grasp. Only then would he risk approaching her. Soon, I would infiltrate Benito's home, where I would protect her with my life.

It wasn't the time to get distracted, and for a fraction of a second, I suffered pangs of regret over what I would be doing later that night and the destruction I would unleash on one arm of the Five Families. The Italian-American Mafia would have been my world, too, if not for Benito Brambilla and my father. As soon as the thought entered my mind, heralding the bitter chill of abandonment, I shut it down. What they'd done, combined with the fact that they'd stolen my position in the Mafia, was why I chose to retaliate. To take back what should have been mine from the start.

My finger curled around the 9mm that was like an extension of my hand. Two men exited the warehouse. Our objective wasn't to kill them all, just enough to make an impact. We weren't there for the men but to destroy what was inside the building. An hour before, a truck had delivered the shipment of opioids and cocaine. With the exit of the driver, we'd waited for the crew remaining in place to guard the building to settle into a false sense of calm.

The last couple of attacks I'd led against Benito had put the boss on alert, but his ego continued to get in the way. He hadn't deviated from his scheduled shipment. He'd increased his guard, but it wasn't enough to stop my team. I had a plan that would bring him and Antonio Caruso to their knees.

It was phase one and would catapult me to the next, an invitation to work for the Brambilla boss himself under the guise of Matteo "Matt" Trambino rather than my rightful name. Max would ring too many bells. He wouldn't know who had stripped him of power until it was too late.

The roar of an engine drew my focus back to the task at hand. Cars started, and the inside crew who hadn't remained past the initial delivery—the time frame when we'd attacked Benito's other warehouse operations—pulled out. We waited to deviate from prior hits, causing unpredictability and confusion.

Our masks were firmly in place. We wouldn't leave anyone standing who could recognize us.

Cristiano was in position on the roof adjacent to the warehouse, taking point as our sniper. He covered the front of the building and the south side, where we didn't have a man in place to watch the windows. No one left behind would escape our ambush. We had planned the raid far in advance, wore tactical gear, and spoke into our earpiece communication devices only when necessary.

My focus sharpened, and adrenaline coursed through me as I balanced on my toes. *Any second now.*

Tommasso gave the first signal, and Cristiano went to work. We waited as he took out the guards stationed within sight. The whiz of the sniper rifle's bullets was music to my ears. Tommasso, Sal, and I hit the ground at a sprint in the darkness of night, converging on the front, side, and back of the dimly lit warehouse. I counted the targets in my head as I eliminated them.

Until then, nature had been on our side with the almost moonless night and whistling winds. We'd hoped to outrun the storm, but we didn't. A flash of light negated the usefulness of our night vision goggles. I pulled mine off and let my eyes adjust.

Lightning split the sky, highlighting our approach but marking our targets as well. The strobe light bisecting the night was too late to save them. The pop of bullets and cries of alarm cut off as more men fell, blanketed under an ominous roll of thunder.

I fired my last bullet then ejected the magazine and slammed another into place in a matter of seconds. More men exited the warehouse, returning fire. Bullets peppered the air around me. One grazed my neck. The resulting burn sent a wave of cold fury that only fueled my determination to take them out.

Through the haze of bloodlust, Tommasso's "clear" registered. Kicking the prone body I'd just shot out of the way, I yanked open the steel door. I took aim and entered the interior as Sal came through the window to my right. Three bodies lay in a growing pool of blood. No others stood in the way of our target.

We weren't in the clear yet. I notched my head at Sal. He took off in the direction I'd indicated—there were offices in the back. Tommasso and I surveyed the tables and pallets teeming with the contraband we sought to destroy. That was his favorite part. Mine was the attack. Sal's "all clear, boss" as he checked the back offices sent a thrill through me.

Cristiano remained on the roof, listening to the police scanners and watching the grid around us. We had time to dismantle the few cameras we hadn't already shot out. In the back offices, Sal worked furiously to wipe all traces of our presence from any recordings. Any images stored elsewhere wouldn't matter—the bulky jackets, indiscernible clothing, gloves, and face masks camouflaged who we were. Our clothes all matched. There were no labels, and the masks had padding sewn in to further obscure the shape of our faces. Black face paint coated our lips where they were visible and around our eyes. The night vision goggles would have been ideal for hiding even more, but they were rendered useless with the light.

We played the long game. Whatever it took. Until we were gone, nothing was removed. No exceptions.

A sense of satisfaction sizzled just beneath my skin. Causing problems for Benito Brambilla was easy. The next day would be another story. The third and fourth parts of my plan were trickier, but I was more than up for a challenge where the reward would punish those who'd wronged my family and taken what should have been mine all along.

I gave the order. "Light it up." I didn't have to see it to know that a wide grin curved Tommasso's mouth. With a rush of heat, his flamethrower sent a stream of fire across the tables in front of him.

Sal emerged from the office as fire consumed the pills, powders, and syringes stacked on the tables. Flames licked the pallets and would soon spread to every inch of wood present in the building. I set C-4 charges to destroy everything inside.

As the inferno progressed, we backtracked to safer ground. The flamethrower winked out, and the three of us hightailed it out of the building. We had about thirty seconds until the first explosion. Sal slapped me on the back as he passed. I slowed until Tommasso joined Sal. I would be the last to exit. Kicking up my pace, I took up the rear as we ran from the warehouse.

A black Lexus screeched to a halt on the block over. Behind tinted windows, Cristiano waited. We arrived at the car, yanked open the doors, and dove in as explosions rocked the night. Cops would be on the scene shortly. As Cristiano peeled away, our guard didn't slip. A false magnetic sheet covered the license plates. We sped through intersections, passing cars, and by some miracle, no cops. A slight veer to the right took us onto the ramp to the streets beneath the city, where we raced through twists and turns at breakneck speed.

Pulling into an underground hotel parking lot, we slid into a spot and killed the engine. We'd taken care of the cameras on the lower level. Even so, we would not use that car again. A gray van pulled up behind us, blocking our car in and further obscuring direct sight. The side door rolled open, and we piled in. John lumbered out of the passenger seat then rounded the front of the van while Nick remained in the driver's seat. John bent down then peeled magnetized license plates from the car, leaving the ones hidden beneath visible, then climbed into the Lexus. He went in one direction, and we went in another, maintaining a moderate speed. John would wipe down, strip, repaint, and sell the car we'd driven.

We didn't speak or remove any article of clothing until we

were topside and the divider was in place to shield us from the front windshield. We stripped out of our masks and black clothes then pulled on jeans and nondescript hoodies. We stored our gear in a hidden compartment behind one of the work shelves that contained carpentry tools.

Dressed, I leaned back against the empty side of the van, my head resting against the metal as the adrenaline released its hold and my body relaxed. With a wide grin, I turned to Sal. "That'll cause an uproar."

"At the very least." Sal agreed. "You ready for tomorrow?"

"You have to ask?" Tommasso laughed. "He was born for this. You, on the other hand, lacked some finesse climbing through the window."

I met Cristiano's gaze while Sal and Tommasso hurled good-natured insults at one another. They were brothers. Cris and I were used to their ways.

When the van slowed, we got out and stepped into a dark alley with no cameras, where Nick left us for the time being. Joe pulled away nice and easy so as not to alert anyone who might have been walking down the sidewalk in front of the alley that he'd stopped at all. We exchanged hushed goodbyes.

As I slipped through a narrow passageway between two businesses, I allowed part of my mind to recap what had gone down. With many of the police force on the payroll for the Mafia, our takedown of Brambilla's warehouse wouldn't make much of a stir and would most likely be reported as faulty wiring. The drugs would never make the news. But what it would do was cut the legs off of Brambilla's operation. Anticipation curled in my gut. The next phase was already in motion.

Benito had arranged a meeting with me. Word had reached his ear about an Italian hit man who delivered results for difficult or troublesome situations. Brambilla would hire me because of my stellar reputation and promises of confidentiality, in the hopes of diminishing any publicity for his crumbling empire.

Miles from the warehouse, I let myself into a lakefront brownstone. I owned the entire building. After dropping the keys on the entryway table, I headed to the kitchen and poured myself a whiskey. Glass in hand, I settled on the couch with the folder of intel I'd collected over the years. I planned to thumb through the documents one last time before my meeting with Brambilla, which I knew would lead to my hire, even though I'd committed the contents of those pages to memory. As I removed the eight-by-ten glossy on the top of the stack, my heart kicked up a notch. I wasn't sure if it was from the image of the woman herself as she laughed with two other Mafia princesses or the knowledge that she would soon be mine to protect.

CHAPTER TWO

LILIANA

"I've got a bad feeling everything is about to change," I said to Sofia, one of my best friends. We'd gone to university together, along with Emiliana and Marissa, the other two in our friend group. I couldn't help the words from manifesting, from finding a voice within the swirling sense of trepidation I'd had since waking. I clutched my cell phone tighter as I crossed the wood planks of my bedroom floor to gaze out the window.

"Why?" Sofia's voice sharpened. Growing up in our world had honed our ability to sense danger from even the most minor nuances. "What happened?"

"I don't trust this line. Dad's been stomping and growling since I woke up. Also, he ordered me to stay home today."

"Ah, okay. Do you want Em and me to come over?"

My fingers curled around the gauzy curtains of my west-facing window in the front of our house. Long shadows stretched over the grand entrance to our luxurious manor as early evening approached. A black Mercedes pulled up. I recognized the model, an S-Class Guard. It was a virtual tank—armored—and whoever owned it had to have been a big deal. I eased back as a tall man unfolded himself from the car.

Mirrored sunglasses obscured his eyes, and a beard covered a portion of his face. As he moved—no, prowled to the front door, my pulse sped in anticipation.

Power rolled off him in waves. He was someone I needed to pay attention to and keep my guard up around because no one my father brought into our home had my best interests at heart, not even dear old Dad.

I snapped a picture and quickly composed a text with a caption asking her to talk to her brother or Enzo and see if they knew anything about him. But that wasn't what I wanted to discuss at the moment, which was why I would send it later.

"Liliana." Sofia pressed.

"Right, sorry. I want you and Emiliana here more than I want my next breath, but I don't think it's a good idea. Something set my dad off." I pictured our encounter that morning, when I'd passed by his office after my morning run. That vein at the side of his head had throbbed, and red had infused his cheeks. Fury crackled in the air around him, and I'd caught myself before I shrank back.

Sofia cleared her throat, bringing me back to the fact that I was on the phone.

"Let's plan to hang out soon." I needed a new subject. "How's Enzo?"

"As gorgeous and unattainable as ever."

"You do know you've had him wrapped around your over-privileged finger since you both were toddlers, right?"

"That doesn't change the fact that he was supposed to marry Elena."

I rolled my eyes, though she couldn't see it. They could have dated since the first year of college. A familiar pang hit me at the thought of school and our friend Marissa, who had been murdered before Christmas break our last year in school. While we led privileged lives, they weren't easy. Death and danger lurked around every unsuspecting corner.

Shaking the memories loose, I turned back to our conversation. Elena Caruso had gone missing when Emiliana had. It was a dark time, one we didn't bring up often. Enzo and Stefano had saved Emiliana, but Elena... we didn't know if she was dead or alive. "Elena has been missing for years. They thought she was killed." I hated saying that, but it was the truth, and Sofia was in her own way when it came to letting herself be happy with Enzo. "The contract can't be valid anymore."

"Nothing's changed. Enzo is slated to be boss, and the contract has been in place since we were children."

The pain in her voice slayed me. "Remember what we always say—"

"—make fate your bitch. Yeah, I haven't forgotten. I'm just out of ideas on what to do in this situation. I mean, if he wanted me, then wouldn't he do something to change his circumstances?"

I worried my lower lip with my teeth, crossing over to my bedroom door and locking it. That man with the beard was in the house, and I wasn't sure why. It made me edgier than I already was. "Let's tackle this small road bump when we get together. We need an epic shopping day."

"And target shooting!" Sofia's tone shifted to her normal happy one. "Em will insist."

"Yeah, she will." We laughed together over that little fact about our bloodthirsty friend. Since college, target practice was one of the things we'd continued, even though Marissa was noticeably absent. After all, being a Mafia princess wasn't a walk in the park. There was backstabbing. We watched out for those who coveted our position in life and our power and did their damnedest to take it from us.

I paused then pulled the phone from my ear to listen. Voices carried not far from my door. "I've got to run, but let's plan on a shopping day." We wrapped up our goodbyes, and she promised to call Em and arrange everything.

After ending the call, I tossed the phone onto the window seat and crossed to my nightstand, where I kept my gun. With the reassuring weight of the weapon in hand, I waited by the side of my bedroom door. Not even two seconds later, a hard rap sounded, followed by one of the guards calling my name.

The need for self-preservation washed over me as I yanked open the door and raised the gun at the same time. I knew which guard it was and longed to put a bullet-sized hole in his forehead for past digressions. One wrong move, and I would do it. Disdain dripped from my voice as I snapped, "What?"

From the corner of my eye, I spotted *him*, the man who had arrived in the black Mercedes. Up close, he was all height, maybe six-two, rippling muscle, and heart-stopping gorgeousness. I gauged who was the bigger threat, known or unknown. The guard I'd dubbed Dumbass sneered. Because of the new guy, he pretended I wasn't serious and faked a laugh as if I was merely playing around. The scar that bisected his chin told another story. He knew firsthand what would happen if he pushed me.

His partner had already paid the price. My father might not have liked me or even treat me well, but no one was allowed to lay a hand on me but him.

Instead of pressing his luck, Dumbass shifted his focus to the new guy in a dismissive she's-not-that-dangerous manner. I was tempted to pull the trigger. My need to end his self-righteous existence was strong, nearly impossible to deny. He was a constant reminder of a terrible day, and I didn't like to think about it. Part of me wondered if my dad would punish me if I did kill the guard. He might. Maybe it wasn't worth it.

"This is Liliana, the boss's daughter and prized possession."

My hand tightened on the 9mm. Dumbass wasn't far off the mark because that's what I was to my father—a possession.

"Dinner is in a half hour. Boss wants you there and on time."

"And if I don't want to go, who's gonna make me?" Cocking

an eyebrow, I let a slow smile pull my lips enough to toe the line between sneering and sweet. Dumbass took the challenge and moved toward me, only to be blocked by the muscleman I had to assume was a new brainless soldier added to Dad's army.

The air crackled with tension. Adonis, the name I assigned to the new guy, stepped forward, stopping Dumbass from getting too close. *Let him try.* It would have ended badly had he done so, just like it had for his friend. I wanted Dumbass to screw up so I could retaliate for what he'd been a part of years ago.

The new guy crossed in front of the guard, effectively blocking him from my sight. The maneuver felt oddly protective and put Adonis directly in my path and very close. The fine hairs all over my body stood at attention, and I had to lock down my muscles to keep from reacting. *Who is this guy?* He didn't seem like the usual fodder of dumb muscle Benito Brambilla—aka dear old Dad, the Brambilla boss—hired.

Dark-gray eyes met mine. I held my ground, refusing to show weakness by shifting back. His arm brushed against mine before he adjusted, creating space between us and shoving Dumbass back another step.

"Dinner is at six," he murmured as he nudged Dumbass away.

My heart thudded, and pings of awareness shot through me. As soon as they were out of sight, I shut and bolted my door, resting my forehead against the cool wood. *What just happened?*

My fingers lingered on the solid door for another second. *Did I literally have a moment with someone in the security detail?* The irony bubbled inside me, and I threw my head back and laughed. *Wouldn't that irritate my father?*

A smile teased my lips, and I pushed away from the door and went into my walk-in closet. Rows of clothes in every shade and style I could ever have wanted hung on display in the changing room. In a slow perusal, my fingers ran across the fabrics as I thought about what to wear.

The dinner I was ordered to attend as a trophy showpiece wasn't anything new. All that was required was a cocktail dress. Normally, I was as conservative in my attire at such things as possible. But in honor of the new soldier, I let myself indulge in something that would turn his head for sure, even though the game I played at was a dangerous one, given my dad's mood earlier.

I pulled a dress from the rack, a black silk number that draped off the hanger with its tight bodice and low-cut V neckline. A band of black crystal beads encircled the waist, and sparkles peppered the flowy material as it fell in waves to midcalf. There was a slit on the right side that would flash a long expanse of leg.

That night, I would be trapped in my own personal hell, entertaining my father's business associates, so I would enjoy myself by tempting the gorgeous new hire. There was no better way to see if he would be a mindless drone or an ally.

If the latter, he would be the only one in our household. The rest were uncaring of my situation or too afraid of my father to hint at going against him in any way.

Around my left thigh, I strapped a sheath then slid a knife inside. Sadly, the dress wasn't one of Sofia's designs, but I would make it work with weapon accessories as best as I could.

As I slipped a delicate gold bracelet on my wrist, the gilded cage I lived in settled around me like an invisible second skin. A ruby pendant nestled between my cleavage. Matching teardrop earrings and deep-red lipstick completed the outfit. My white-blond hair fell in loose waves around my shoulders. A dab of perfume, a hint of mascara, and smoky-black eyeliner were the only other concessions I chose to highlight my features. I stood before the floor-length mirror wearing black Louboutins, the red soles visible when I pivoted to the side.

With a critical eye, I scrutinized my outfit. Mafia royalty reflected back. I tilted my chin in silent acknowledgment, ready for the next battle, which would be on my terms.

In a swirl of silk, I left my room, my heels clicking against the wood floors. As I descended the stairs, my gaze swept over the visible portion of the first floor, cataloging any threats. My heart sank as my father paused at the landing, where he made a show of looking at his watch then back to me. A pain pierced my heart, and I pulled in a slow breath, suppressing my feelings like I always did. Our relationship would never be what I wished it would.

His black suit jacket strained against the swell of his belly. A cold smile pulled his thin lips back, and no warmth lurked in his dead eyes as he offered his elbow. I slipped my hand into the crook of his arm, and we moved into the dining room, where several men mingled.

My back stiffened, and masked fury radiated from my father at the sight before us. Either I was late, or they were early. I straightened my shoulder and held my head high as we walked into the dining room together. Three sets of men turned at our entrance, and I worked hard to keep my face impassive. They weren't the other bosses, as I'd expected, but rivals from the cartel. *What the hell is going on?*

Leonardo, my father's underboss, his second-in-command, was the third man present. What I found interesting was that Dino, Dad's advisor, wasn't at the meeting. Leonardo and Dino were at the top tier of the Brambilla empire, sitting just below my dad. They should both have been in attendance if any major moves were being made. Knowing Dino, I bet he didn't approve of their latest maneuver.

I accepted a glass of wine from one of the servers then took a much needed sip. Without telegraphing what I was doing, I checked the guards stationed at the two exits. Dad touched my arm, pulling my focus back, then made introductions. Cold, dead eyes gazed back at me as Raphe, the cartel boss, closed his hand around mine. My skin crawled at his touch. As soon as I was able, I pulled my hand free.

"And this is my son, Jose." Raphe indicated with a wave of his hand.

My smile was frozen as Jose stepped forward and did a slow perusal from my head to my toes and back up again. Revulsion churned in my gut as he took my hand and lingered. When he glided his thumb over the top of my fingers in a back and forth caress, I yanked it back.

Leonardo nodded in my direction, and I offered a neutral greeting to him as well. Not a fan. Neither of us was fond of one another. That didn't matter, though. It was talk to him or to the two guests who made me incredibly uncomfortable.

When there was a little space between Leonardo and the cartel men, I turned to him to try to get some information. "Leo, did you arrange this evening?"

Thin lips lifted in a mocking grin. "Do you find our guests distasteful?"

My brows rose. *Bold.* I couldn't figure out what the game plan was. "I'm not here to pass judgment."

"Of course not. You're decoration."

"And you're only here to even the odds."

His face went from pasty to tomato red as his anger got the best of him.

It was clear that I wasn't going to get anything out of him, but I did feel better insulting his worth. He was just an extra body to even our side against the cartel's.

With my only choice to continue to be insulted by Leonardo, I changed gears to brave the waters with Raphe's son, Jose. As soon as I crossed the room to him, that earlier gleam flared up, and I had to repress a shiver, reminding myself that he couldn't touch me. That would have been a direct insult to my father, whose motto was "look all you want, but touch and pay with your life."

It would have been nice if his motives were from love. They weren't. It was all about what I could bring to him.

"Liliana," Jose purred my name—*gross*. "I hear you recently graduated college."

"Yes. I'm still adjusting to being back home. It's very different from living at school."

"I'm sure there were many parties you went to. Lots of drinking. Party drugs."

The mention of party drugs made my hand tighten on the glass of wine I held. "There were parties, but drugs aren't my thing." When his dad asked me a question, I forced myself to set my glass on the table by my elbow before I gulped the entire thing down. I needed to pay attention to my surroundings, not overindulge in wine. This was not the time or place.

Without looking at Jose, I could feel his eyes on me, and the fine hair on the back of my neck rose, my fight-or-flight instincts barely contained. There was something unsettling about the way he watched me.

When Raphe caught my eye, I pivoted and joined his conversation with my dad, effectively bypassing Jose. Leonardo could talk with him. They were both weasels. I was sure they had plenty in common.

As I moved through the room, making small talk with the men, I snuck glances at Adonis. He'd perfected that trick of looking stoic while observing everything around him. I could tell because it's something I did as well.

Not long after talking to Raphe and another pass at Leonardo, I moved back to where my wine was. Jose was nearby, and I gave him what I hoped passed as a smile and reached for the glass. Before I could lift it to my lips, Adonis was there, taking the wine before I could take a drink.

"Let me get you a new glass." His words were low and threatening. Jose held his eyes before shrugging and walking away. Then the soldier turned to me, whispering near my ear as he passed by for the kitchen. "He spiked your drink. I'll watch them, but don't set your drink down or turn your attention from it. If you need a refill or someone to hold it for you, I'll handle it."

My body trembled, and I clasped my hands together to hide it. The soldier brought a fresh drink, but I was so shaken that I didn't consume any. It wasn't that I didn't trust him, especially after what he'd done, but that I was terrified of what could have happened. And my father... after what he had done to my mother the last year I had with her, I wasn't sure that he wasn't in on it. It was another indication that I needed to move out. If I could have left, I would have, but he would never let me go unless he married me to gain a vital connection. I narrowed my gaze at Raphe and Jose. *What can my father gain from selling me out to them?*

It wasn't long before we took our seats around the ornate dining room table. Fine china and crystal goblets were before us as the staff brought in course after course.

Each minute of the evening passed in painful slowness. After declining dessert, I knew I had only seconds until I was free. Dad invited the men into the study to discuss business over brandy or something equally repulsive. I prayed they didn't add me to the list of topics to barter over.

I rose from the table, judging whether the best route was past the cartel guys or Leonardo. I chose the lesser of two evils, the known threat—Leonardo.

I shifted to the right as everyone gained their feet. Excusing myself, I was at the doorway where the new guard was stationed, his eyes forward. The hair on the back of my neck stood, and I knew without looking that Jose was hot on my heels.

As I crossed the threshold from the dining room to the hallway, the new soldier stepped in front of the doorway, blocking Jose's path. *Interesting.* I glanced over my shoulder, never slowing my steps, to see the soldier's impenetrable stance. As Jose was called to join the others, my protective soldier turned and followed me. Our gazes locked and held, and my footing faltered. In long strides, he closed the distance between us then gestured for me to continue.

I bristled at his nearness, my emotions at war with what he represented, and the contradiction of his actions. *Does he pity me?* He'd certainly seen enough. I wasn't weak. All he had to do was ask Dumbass. His scar spoke for itself.

Still, wariness swam through me, and a part of me hoped that I was wrong about the man being another cog in my dad's employ. He'd looked after me, and that alone should have told me that he was trustworthy. But trust was hard to come by in life. "Thank you for what you did earlier. Twice, actually. But I don't need an escort."

A dark brow rose, somehow only enhancing his features. "Someone needs to accompany you. No one else is up for the job."

The deep cadence of his voice sent goose bumps dancing along my skin. Head high, I kept pace beside his longer strides until we were at my room. Without saying a word, I went in and shut the door behind me, slamming home the lock. A lone thought trailed after his words. He wasn't wrong—I did need protection. My situation was precarious and inescapable.

CHAPTER THREE

MAX

My mind whirled with thoughts of Liliana. After last night's train wreck of a dinner, I'd made sure she got to her room safely. The thought of that cartel asshole drugging her sent rage through me. It had taken everything I had to keep the interaction discreet.

That should have been the last of my interactions with her that evening, but it wasn't. I couldn't exorcise her from my dreams. The way that dress clung to her in all the right places... and the fear and sadness in her blue eyes at what had almost happened. She slipped past my defenses, and I longed to hold her. I had felt a connection for a long time, since her Sicilian grandfather, Vincenzo, had shared reports from his private investigator, where I'd come to know her, at least on paper. And the pictures paled in comparison to being in her presence. The fantasies in my dreams of her bled into the present, which wasn't ideal.

It was inevitable that I'd grown close to Liliana. It wasn't expected. The fact that she was beautiful, kind, and loyal to those she cared for meant something to me. But it was her relationship with Benito that tied us together and made me want to fight for her, to be her champion.

Her father treated her as only a little better than the soldiers in his employ, if not slightly less than. There was no love lost between the two. I could practically see how much she longed for things to be different, her abandonment issues clear as day. I had battled similar experiences. I understood her, and with each passing hour, I'd grown to respect her strength.

I had to remain focused. My endgame was within sight and getting closer with every bit of trust I gained from the Brambilla boss.

Ruthlessly, I shoved the feisty princess from my mind and headed to Benito's office for a mandatory meeting. There had been another hit to one of his warehouses the night before. It hadn't been my crew, but they'd been in place, watching who did. Word was out that Brambilla's empire was weakening, and it was making him careless and desperate. I had the intel I needed to establish that without me, Benito's business would crumble.

At the entrance to the sprawling manor were two stationed guards. The home consisted of old-world and dark architecture, arched doorways and windows, rough-hewn beams bisecting the celling, matte browns and tans for the walls, and cream-colored silk drapes that pooled on the wood floors.

I passed by the soldiers with a slight nod in acknowledgment. We'd met the other day, and they'd been instructed as to who I was but not told my purpose for working with the boss. Benito wouldn't have wanted the threat to his power to get out, even though it had leaked. The hit the night before was proof. That was our doing, and the news hadn't traveled far yet. Only a select few knew the extent of damage the attacks had caused to the Brambilla empire and what would happen if they continued.

The dinner with the cartel boss was Benito's mistake and a

key step toward his downfall. Between the two factions, alliances were made. He seemed to think the cartel would provide added protection and an influx of drugs to cover what had been lost in previous raids. Everything came with a price, and I wondered if he'd realized what his would be.

I knew it would cost him his daughter. Then his empire.

Once past the entryway, I ran my hand along my jawline. The beard I'd grown for my trip to America was thick, and I wanted to trim it, but it helped to hide my face enough from those who weren't ready to learn the truth of who I was.

Benito's office was in the southwest area of the house. To reach the hallway that would take me there, I would have had to pass by the three seasons room, where I knew Liliana liked to have her morning coffee.

I glanced at my watch. There was time. Sunlight bounced around the room from the wall-to-wall windows. There was a hanging basket seat surrounded by plants and several inviting chairs and couches. But the woman reclining on the oversized chair, her stiletto-clad feet on the ottoman and a cup of coffee paused halfway to her mouth, drew all my focus. I leaned against the side of the opened French doors, my gaze leisurely traveling around the room when all I wanted to do was get to know her better.

"Can I help you?" Her brows arched over arresting bluish-purple eyes that reminded me of a tanzanite stone.

"We weren't properly introduced. I lived in Sicily until recently. I'm Matteo Trambino, but you can call me Matt." It was odd to use the alias rather than my given name, but Matt and Max were close enough that I wouldn't have a delayed response to someone calling me the other name. Before I could stop myself, I glanced at her mouth then forced myself to meet her gaze. That wasn't why I was there. "I have a meeting with the boss. But I was curious. Your dad treats you like a porcelain doll, but that guard... didn't."

A smirk pulled at her pink lips. "Why are you curious? I thought you had a brain." She stood and walked toward me, pausing when we were side by side. "Don't disappoint me."

We locked gazes, and I held her in place with the intensity I felt inside of me at the wrongness of what I'd witnessed. "And the dinner guests? There was an undercurrent there that wasn't shut down." I couldn't say what I wanted or that her father hadn't stopped it. The interactions I'd noticed didn't fit with the intel I'd studied while in Italy.

She lifted her shoulders in a casual shrug that belied the fury and pain flaring in her eyes. "I'm a means to an end. Property." She leaned in close, her light and airy scent swirling around me. "Don't think you can jump on the asshole train with the rest of his soldiers." She winked. "I'm always prepared."

I grinned when I felt the press of her blade at my femoral artery, my body reacting in ways it shouldn't have. But it was the Mafia, and the threat of the knife was foreplay. "Wouldn't dream of it."

When her touch fell away, I wanted to pull her back into my arms, risking whatever danger she would bring with the action. I wanted her, and that wasn't going away.

The click of her heels echoed along the hallway as she left. My gaze followed the intoxicating sway of her hips until she was out of sight. Pushing off the doorjamb, I headed for Brambilla's office, Liliana still in the forefront of my thoughts. At least part of my plan would be a challenge. What was already in motion was child's play.

Getting my head back in the game, I hardened my heart to Liliana's plight and zeroed in on the partially open solid wood door that led into Brambilla's office. I rapped my knuckles and schooled my features to hide the bloodlust that threatened to overtake me. It wasn't the time. There was so much more that needed to be put into place before the final blow was dealt.

"Come in," Benito said with a grunt.

I entered the plush office with its continuation of deep reds, tans, and browns. His desk was an overlarge piece of furniture, heavy and ornate. The room was thick with the sweet scent of cigar smoke, even though he didn't have one burning. Behind the desk, dark beady eyes met mine in a wash of calculated manipulation. Liliana looked nothing like him, instead resembling her mother.

At first glance, someone might have thought Benito was too focused on enjoying pasta, wine, and cigars. Looking closer showed how devoid of warmth his eyes were. Power didn't cling to him in the way it should have, but greed and ruthlessness did. I would not underestimate him. Instead, I would deliver my final blow when I had him by the balls.

Anger crackled through the air. "What did you find out?"

That was my cue. "The attack the other night was ordered by associates of Raphe Espinosa's cartel. It was a two-part strike meant to weaken you and force your hand. I would guess they want to further exploit your need to replenish the loss in your distribution, and by the son's interest at dinner last night, perhaps Liliana to cement their way into the family."

A low growl slipped through his lips. "This changes everything. I want you to stick to Liliana like glue."

"I wasn't brought on to be a glorified guard." I'd left the door ajar, and the faint click of heels tapping against the wood floor was getting louder. Eventually, I would let Liliana know why I was there. We were due for another talk. And if she heard something through the open door, I expected her curiosity to get the better of her, which would reveal more information from Benito.

Benito slapped the flat of his hand onto the desk with a resounding crack. "You will do it. Today, I will send soldiers to Raphe's door, breaking off the deal in a manner that will leave no doubt in his mind that I know what went down at my warehouse. If Liliana is his target, he will not succeed. I have other uses for my daughter."

The clicks stopped, and I waited for the pending explosion. I wasn't disappointed when she slapped her hand against the door, pushing it wide.

"Excuse me? What did I overhear about you referencing my usefulness?" Fury vibrated from her pinched mouth, but she caught her reaction and quickly schooled her features to appear calm and distant, almost uncaring. If one missed the way her hands trembled before she hid them in the folds of her skirt or the way her expressive eyes looked dead inside, her façade was believable.

I leaned back to remove myself from the path of her animosity. Liliana wasn't the only one who carefully camouflaged her disdain. Benito also echoed his outrage with clenched fists and a high color infusing his ruddy cheeks. "There will be another dinner tonight. An essential one." Benito's tone left no room for questions.

Instead of watching him, I focused on her. I could feel myself softening toward her, which was a deadly game at that point in my plan, something I couldn't afford. Through Liliana's grandfather's information, I knew enough about the murder of Benito's wife. Both she and the daughter had been the target, but Liliana had survived. *Why, then, do these two despise one another?*

Liliana tilted her chin, and her long blond hair shifted, falling over her left shoulder in a mass of light-catching waves. "I have plans."

"Cancel them." Benito snapped. "You need to be here, dressed appropriately and greeting our guests by six. Not a second past that." His head notched in my direction. "Matt here will be shadowing you and will drag you back if necessary."

Liliana's head jerked as if slapped. "What's the point in acting as hostess, as the doting daughter, when I mean next to nothing to you?"

25

"That's where you're wrong, Lilianna." Benito leaned back against his chair, a smirk pulling his lips to one side. "You're the key to my dynasty, and you'll do what's asked of you."

CHAPTER FOUR

MAX

Benito didn't disappoint, I would give him that. He stayed true to character, showing his daughter how little he cared about her. In that moment, I didn't think I'd ever hated him more.

Liliana whirled on her heels and took off down the hall. I followed.

"Where the hell are you going?" Benito snapped.

Asshole. "I'm following orders and sticking to her like glue." I didn't wait for a response but hurried after her. I rounded the corner, waiting until I was out of direct earshot of Benito, who had probably returned to his office. "Lil, wait."

She paused and turned to me. I jogged the rest of the way to catch up. The nickname had slipped, but that was a good thing, as it caught her attention. "Are you okay?"

Her eyes narrowed, fury swirling in their blueish-purple depths. "What do you think?"

"I'm not going to let anything happen to you." Beneath the anger, hurt pulsed like a beacon. I couldn't ignore her pain.

"There's nothing you can do." Her words were whispered.

"You would be surprised." I shouldn't have said it, but I did.

She needed me in her corner, even though it wasn't possible to share everything, I could give her a sense of security.

"What do you want?"

That was a loaded question. I wanted a lot of things, and soothing her hurt was one of them. *Do people only take from her? Has no one given freely, made her feel special?* My gaze dropped to her lips then jerked back up. "I was thinking we could get out of here. At least for a little while."

When her head tilted to the side, observing me with new interest, I wanted to smack myself in the forehead. That sounded like I was asking her on a date. If I could have invited her out, I would have, but that didn't fall in line with the role I had to play. "Maybe you want to meet your friends? Anything to get out of this place and away from..." I let the rest hang. I couldn't push things too far. Not yet.

The anger was back, crackling with a heated intensity. "Oh, I'm definitely getting out of here."

With her cryptic promise, she whirled around and hurried off in the direction of her room. The tension that lived between my shoulders only increased. She was planning something. Whatever it was, I would be by her side, one way or another.

Liliana

A scream built, begging for release as it beat against the back of my throat. With Herculean effort, I shoved it down, as I always did. The conversation with my father had me seriously rattled. I had to get out of there. And my new security detail—Matt, aka Adonis—had witnessed the whole thing. Lovely.

Maybe that wasn't something to be horrified about. He'd shown kindness in coming after me, and it had almost seemed like he'd asked me on a date. If I had been so upset, I would have entertained that he had. But from what my dad had said, my life wasn't my own. He controlled my future.

Times like those, I missed Mom the most. My fingers grazed the diamond earrings she'd loved that had been a gift from her mom and which she'd given to me that last year, saying that I was more priceless than anything else. It was a piece of her that she wanted me to have always, no matter what.

Maybe she knew something bad was coming—just not what or when.

Ahh. The memories hurt more than helped. I had to do something, get away for a little while. What I needed were Sofia and Emiliana, my two best friends who were there for me, no matter what—especially after what we'd gone through in our last year in college when Marissa was murdered. The tragedy had brought us closer together, and an unbreakable pact was formed.

My heels struck the wood floors, echoing the helplessness thrumming through me as I walked with purpose back to my room. Once inside, I slammed and locked the door. I stabbed Emiliana's contact info with my index finger then the speaker button before dropping the phone onto an oversized chair in my dressing room. Clothes in every hue and style surrounded me. Shoes lined one side from top to bottom. I snagged a pair of red-soled Louboutins then ran my fingers along the shirts on the opposite wall until I found what I wanted.

I couldn't stand still. Like a caged animal, I paced. The walls of my spacious bedroom were closing in. I peeled off my shirt and the flowy skirt I had worn when I thought it would be a relatively calm day. I had been dead wrong.

"Hey, Lil." Em's throaty voice purred over the line, and a part of me settled.

I needed my girls with me at least until I had to return for that joke of a dinner I was being forced to attend. "We need to meet. Lunch. Shopping. Bitching. I need you and Sofia sooner rather than later."

"On it. I'll get Sof, and we'll meet you at our favorite outdoor café on the north side."

"I'll be there in half an hour."

After disconnecting, I grabbed a dark-red silk shirt that dipped low and stretchy black pants with a plethora of pockets that I painted on my body. A rose-gold layered choker that followed the deep-V neckline was next. Then I compulsively touched Mom's diamond earrings again, assuring myself they were still there. Having something of hers with me when I was off-balance always helped. Even though I would trade them—or anything, really—to have just one more day with her.

I would never forget the time we lay in the grass when I was young and she'd said, "Sometimes a gentle soul is born into a dark existence. The key is to find ways to nurture it while coexisting." It was a reminder to always find something good to be thankful for. Possessions didn't matter. The people we loved did. She'd been my world before everything had gone dark. I was lucky to have Emiliana and Sofia.

On an exhale I shook off the melancholy vibe that had descended. It wasn't the time to reminisce or think about what-ifs.

Turning from side to side, I scrutinized the image reflected at me. The silk blouse was trendy and highlighted all the right curves, emphasizing my small waist where it stopped at the top of my black pants. The heels gave me the height I lacked while adding emphasis to my legs.

I picked up a brush and ran it through my hair until it shone in platinum waves, falling more than halfway down my back. I touched up the smoky eyeliner with a deft hand and added another swipe of mascara to my lashes, making my blue eyes stand out even more. I applied a quick coat of lipstick then dropped the tube and my phone into the leather clutch that

NO WAY OUT

contained a knife and my credit cards. I was ready to go. With
determined strides, I went to my bedroom door, flipped the
lock, and wrenched it open.

Matt blocked my way, as I knew he would. He was to be
glued to me, per my father's orders. If he had been one of the
other guards, I would have sneered and made a derogatory
watchdog comment, followed with a taunt asking if they liked
what they saw. They might have replied or leered, but after
what had happened with the one I refused to name and Dumbass, they knew they couldn't touch me.

With Matt, I did none of those things. He was... different.
The fire that burned in my gut told me how much. It was crazy,
but I wanted him to touch me. The instant flare in his graphite
gaze and the dilated pupils made me think he wanted to do the
same.

"Princess." He nodded then settled a large hand on the small
of my back. "Where to?"

I repressed the shiver that followed in the wake of his sinful
voice and the electrifying touch of his hand. The way he
crowded me felt protective instead of annoying. We passed by a
mirror, and I had to do a double take. He was curved toward me
as if he was a human shield. My heart skipped a beat.

With effort, I shoved the impossible attraction aside.
Nothing would come of it. My father owned him, as he did me.
I didn't know what Matt had done to sell his soul to the devil,
but he was in his employ, which meant he was not for me.

My craptastic mood came back with the power of a freight
train as the reason why I had to get out of the house returned.
The evil glint in my father's eye as he told me I was the key to
his dynasty made me nauseous. The emphasis on tonight's
guests was the nail in my looming coffin. Whatever he planned
—and I seriously hoped it wasn't who he would marry me off to
—was going down this evening.

The silence Matt maintained when I didn't respond to his

question about where we were going helped. We made our way through the house then past the connecting door to the garage that housed half a dozen cars. My heels clicked against the painted cement floor until I came to the black Aston Martin convertible. When I reached for the door, Matt's hand clamped over mine. He pulled me against his side then led me around the car to the passenger's seat.

"It doesn't work that way, Princess." His deep voice unleashed a volley of intoxicating sensations dancing along my skin.

The way he held me against his body sent a jolt of desire to my core, and I sank my teeth into my bottom lip to keep from moaning. It'd been too long since I'd let a man touch me. That needed to change, and soon.

From beneath my lashes, I snuck a peek at him. His beard had to have been covering an angular jaw. I wanted to ask him to shave so that I could see it. Although the thought of what those whiskers would feel like...

My fingers twitched as I imagined brushing my thumb across his firm lips. Something told me he would have to be in control. Besides, if I slept with him, I would be breaking my rule of never letting the guards touch me or get too close. It would inevitably give the others ideas and my father an even greater stronghold over my life—after he killed the guard. I felt caged as it was. I didn't need to give him a way to strengthen the bars that held me.

Matt leaned over me, fastening my seat belt.

I scowled, determined to ignore the intoxicating scent of his cologne. "Enjoy the small amount of control you have. It won't last."

"You going to make things difficult for me?" His lips twitched as he turned his head, inches from my face.

A wicked thrill raced through me. "Very." A slow grin curved my mouth at the thought of how pissed my dad would be if I got involved with his newest soldier. *Why not muddy up the waters a little?* I was no fool. The plans he had for me had to do with selling me off to the highest bidder. With a tilt of my head, I subtly inched closer.

Our lips were centimeters apart, and I dropped my gaze to them, wondering if he would do anything. When he straightened, a surge of disappointment had me frowning. I needed to get a grip.

I settled in as he rounded the car then got into the driver's seat. The engine purred to life, and we were off. With the top down, a false sense of freedom spiked in my blood. I was meeting my girls, my crew from college and mutual prisoners in the Mafia world. If I was reading the writing on the wall correctly, I was pretty sure I would need their help sooner rather than later.

Whether I wanted to admit it or not, I needed them. I couldn't shake the sense of impending doom from my last encounter with Dad. I flipped on the radio, letting Ava Max's "Kings & Queens" blast through the open interior of the car. *Fitting.*

From the corner of my eye, I checked out Matt as he maneuvered the high-performance car out of my neighborhood and onto the highway that would take us to Michigan Avenue and my friends. Not for the first time, a tingle of awareness coursed through me. The timeless question of friend or foe ran through my mind, and I replayed our every interaction.

"Do you like working for my father?" I don't know why I asked that. Maybe I hoped he would say no. But then again, I didn't want him to leave.

"It's a job, and I'll see it through." He glanced at me, and I frowned. "Your home is different than what I'm used to. Where I grew up, there was always laughter and so much cooking. When I watch you and Benito interact, I wish that I could transport you to where I lived." He shrugged. "I mean no disrespect."

"None taken. Ever since Mom was killed, our lives have changed drastically." I let silence settle around us again, content and comfortable in his presence.

"Do you have any other family close by? Or in Italy?"

"No. I mean, yes, I have family in Italy, but there's bad blood between us."

A few beats passed before he responded. "I'm sorry to hear that."

I shrugged. Nothing could be done. The miles kept the distance between us and them.

As he flew down the highway then wove through the city streets, I made my decision. I would treat him as an ally. God knew I needed one in that mausoleum. Not only that, but he had looked out for me at that dinner. Drugs and I would never mix, not after the addiction my mom struggled with. Still, it had to have bothered Matt that he was ordered to shadow me, especially when I got the vibe that he was more than a mere foot soldier.

As we neared the café where I would meet Emiliana and Sofia, I turned in my seat to watch his reactions to my question. "Is this what you aspired to while working with my father? Being a glorified babysitter?"

He turned his head from the road, casting me a glance. An amused grin had curved his lips, and I couldn't help but drop my gaze to them. "Is that what you think I'm doing?"

"Pretty much." I faced forward once more, finding the high-end stores that we passed safer to gaze at than the visage of the powerful man beside me. "I have a feeling you do other work for my father, and playing guard dog to a mafia princess is not one of your usual duties."

"I wasn't aware you were interested in how I spend my days. Or nights."

I repressed a shiver at the way his deep voice had lowered a fraction, fairly purring over the word "nights." In an attempt to appear unaffected, I smirked, all the while fighting the cauldron of desire that sparked to life in my core. *Who is this guy?* "I'm not interested. Not like that. But you're different than his other soldiers."

"Why do you say 'his soldiers'? As his daughter, they answer to you too."

I knew I was right about him being different. He held himself apart, even in that question. And not only that, but my father had included him in a discussion that he would have kicked most of the men out of so he could humiliate me in private.

I shrugged in response to Matt's inquiry. No need to explain the hierarchy in our house or that my father had wished I had been the one to die all those years ago. In a way, we both did.

Done with the conversation, I turned up the radio then tapped my nail on the armrest, impatient to see my friends. A small smile curved my face as we drew up to the café, where they waited at an outdoor table. Sofia's long hair fell in mahogany waves over her shoulder. Her lips pursed, and she lowered her sunglasses as Matt maneuvered us into a parking spot not far from where they sat. My hand curled around the door handle as his gripped my wrist, locking me in place.

I whipped around. The familiar lick of fear that usually crawled over my skin from someone grabbing me like that was surprisingly absent. My lips parted to snap at him, but he beat me to it.

"Wait for me to open the door."

His gray eyes burned into mine with that same possessiveness from earlier and stole my breath. I managed a slight nod then waited for him to round the car. When he opened my door, he extended a hand to me while continuing to scan the area.

I placed my palm in his. That spark of awareness from his touch infused my blood. *Does he feel it too?* He drew me to him with a light tug, closed and locked the car, then released me.

Side by side, we made our way along the walkway mere feet from Emiliana and Sofia. The heat from his hand at my back comforted me.

With each step, people parted to move out of our way. I lived for such moments when I could get out from under my father's thumb and be temporarily freed from my gilded cage. I held my head higher, the headiness of experiencing the power that bled from him intoxicating. I needed more of that. Out of the house, I could wield it, but not within. I was royalty, after all, and the city knew it.

CHAPTER FIVE

LILIANA

M y friends watched our approach. Emiliana tensed, but
Sofia swept her gaze in a slow perusal over Matt. I
stiffened as jealousy burned in the wake of her appreciative
grin. Staking a claim, for a reason I couldn't fathom, I let the
palm of my hand closest to Matt brush over his thigh. I felt his
attention, the intensity of his focus, without having to turn my
head to know he was looking at me.

I said nothing, but the message was clear to both of my
friends. He was mine, even though I didn't know in precisely
what way I wanted him. Well, I did, but it couldn't happen.
Right?

I dropped my clutch on the table and sat down. Matt faded
into the background along with my friends' guards, and the
girls' gazes returned to me. The waiter appeared a second later
and took our orders. After he left, the inquisition began.

"Is that the new soldier?" Emiliana bristled, her fist clenching, and I knew she wanted the weighty reassurance of her gun.
New members of our security detail caused her anxiety, stem-
ming from past trauma. "What do you know about him?"

I shrugged, turning to Sofia with raised brows. "Other than

his name, I know the same amount of details as you. Weren't you going to ask your brother about him? Or Enzo? Did you find anything out?"

The slight pinch to Sofia's features didn't go unnoticed, but neither Em nor I said anything. Why she and Enzo were at odds would be brought up. Sofia had been in love with Em's brother since we were toddlers. But like everything in our world, it was complicated.

I wasn't surprised that Sofia had gone to her brother Marco for information, as she was tight with all three of them. Marco was the underboss to her dad, fierce, and a total manwhore. We loved him anyway.

Our voices were hushed, and we leaned forward enough to keep what we said for our ears only. Sofia smirked, and a ripple of excitement shot through me. Knowledge was power, and I needed to know everything I could to stay on top of my father's plans, whatever nightmare scenario he might have had in store.

The waitstaff swooped in and deposited our salads, refilled our wineglasses, then left as silently as they'd come.

"I didn't get much." Sofia's gold bangle bracelets jingled as she reached for her wine. "Based on the name you gave me, my brother said Matteo Trambino is a hitman who works for the original families. He's well known and gets the job done."

"The Sicilians? Shit." I couldn't wrap my head around it. "Who is my dad planning on taking out, and why is Matt guarding me? That wouldn't fit into a hitman's job description."

"No. My guess is there's either a contract out on you or Benito is using him for a show of strength." Em drummed her fingers against the table, drawing my gaze to her short, torn fingernails. "We need to figure out which one it is."

I snuck a glance at him over my shoulder. It took me a minute to pick him out from the other patrons, staff, and plants that surrounded the outer edges of the patio. When I faced my friends again, determination hardened my features. "I'll find out on the way home. He's"—I struggled to define what he truly was to me—"an ally of sorts."

Sofia threw her head back and laughed, garnering the admiration of several nearby men. Gorgeous and sexy, she was noticed by everyone. There was more talent in her little pinky than most people have in their whole body, and it shone from deep inside her, making others want to bask in her good fortune. That was until they found out she'd slit their throat without remorse if the situation called for it. She was a complete contradiction, and I got why that was alluring. "A bedroom ally?"

I shrugged. Sadly, it wasn't like that. "He makes me feel safe at home."

The laughter died an instant death from Sof's full lips at that comment. She reached over and squeezed my hand while Em continued to stab her salad with her fork. "Then I'm glad he's here too."

"What's going on that you're so on edge?" Em set her fork down, pushing her mostly finished meal aside.

"The ridiculous dinner parties my dad keeps throwing."

"Ah, the ones where your presence is required? In a show of femininity and what they can't have?"

"Mm-hmm." I nodded. "It's nothing new, only I can feel the noose tightening. There's this expectation in the air all the time now that for the right price, arrangements could be made—and by that, I mean marriage to increase his reach, money, favors... I don't know what he's looking for, precisely." I swallowed hard to keep the bile down.

"He's dead," Sof growled. "I'll tell Marco. Maybe he can do something."

No one could. My eyes misted. I loved them so much. Sof's kind heart and Em's viciousness slayed me. Even though we were from different factions within the five families, I would give my life for them, and I knew they would do the same.

"Shake it off, Lil." Em's voice was brittle, reminding me of how much worse she'd had it at one point in her life. "We all have our demons."

On an exhale, Sofia pushed aside her sympathy with a resigned, "It's how we chose to go on—"

"And execute them." Em winked.

All three of us laughed. *If only.* "And on that note. I'm pretty sure that the dinner guests tonight will be Antonio Caruso and his son."

"Tony," Em spat.

"Yep." A rush of hatred burst through my veins. The surge of fury matched my friends' expressions in the way their eyes flashed and fists curled. We'd grown up together. Her father wasn't the kindest, either. "I'm going to get him alone and make him admit he was the one who murdered Marissa."

"And if we're right," Sofia said, "that puts you at risk. We can't have that. Invite us over."

"Not exactly at risk." Em lowered her voice to a whisper. "Matt."

"True. He'll be there. I should be fine. If Tony makes a move to harm me, Matt will end him."

"An underboss?" Sofia's brows rose.

She had a point. There were rules. "I'll figure something out. But we need proof. Then we need to make him pay."

"Lil?"

I jerked, and my elbow bumped the back of my chair as my gaze fell on the curvy brunette approaching our table. "Eva?"

"Hey, cuz." She came to my side and hugged me. Pulling a chair out, she fell into the seat, her shopping bags falling to the ground beside her. "Sofia. Emiliana. What's going on?"

"I didn't know you were back." Sofia pointed to Eva's bags as the waitstaff swept in and delivered a glass of wine to Eva. "What'd you get?"

"I thought you weren't coming back for a month." Last I'd

talked to my cousin, she'd planned on going to Sicily and sleeping her way through Italy. "Are you here by yourself?"

Eva's pouty red lips pursed, and she shrugged. "I was supposed to shop with Mirra, but she bailed last minute. So... what could I do?"

"When the urge hits..." Sofia's eyes sparkled. Our resident shopaholic.

"Exactly." Eva nodded. "What're you all doing for the rest of the day? Want to go to the lake house?"

I wanted to shrink in my seat. We'd gone to the lake house in the past, but everything was on a grand scale with Eva. I felt inadequate in her presence. She was outgoing, gorgeous, and had an enviable hourglass figure. I paled in comparison, literally. With my lackluster blond hair, pale skin—*I'm Italian, for God's sake*—and slender build, I wasn't turning any heads. I could fill out a bathing suit, but not like her.

Plus, I was content to hang with Em and Sofia, where I was happiest. Eva had a sense of freedom about her that I never would. My dad siphoned any power I could have, and freedom was an illusion in my world. She didn't have the same target on her back.

The best years of my life were after Mom was murdered and I was away at college with Sofia, Emiliana, Marissa, and several of our cousins, including Eva. I missed those days with a fierceness that cast a bleak hue on the future with my father at the helm.

"I can't." the words burst from my lips, followed by a sense of relief. "There's a dinner at the house. I'm supposed to be there for it."

"Ah, I heard about that." Eva swirled her wine then took a sip. "I ran into Tony coming out of the bank. He mentioned that's where he would be this evening when I suggested getting everyone together at the beach."

"Did he say what tonight was about?" Emiliana asked, and I could have kissed her.

I desperately wanted confirmation about why but didn't want to shed light onto how bad it was at home with my dad leaving me out of the plan for the evening. Pity wasn't something I wanted to see reflected on my friends' faces. And my cousin... I had a feeling she would revel in it, given that occasional hard glint that entered her sultry brown eyes. She also thought our lives were so much better than hers as she was only a cousin, not Mafia royalty. It wasn't true. Marissa and I'd had home environments that weren't as loving as Emiliana's and Sofia's.

Eva wasn't typically over. My dad didn't have time for "noisy kids"—irritating young adults—and preferred that I met my friends or female cousins out shopping or at restaurants, which had always been fine with me. In public, he was the doting and protective Mafia boss and loving father.

Eva waved the waiter over for a refill before she addressed Em's question. "No, he was distracted. He just said it was business. And you know me. I'm out for a good time. Leave the business aspects to them. God, I miss Marissa."

Sofia choked on her wine. Em pounded her on the back, a calculating gleam entering her dark eyes that zeroed in on Eva. "Sometimes I forget how close you and Marissa were."

"Christ." I wasn't expecting Marissa's name spoken aloud, and with it, the onslaught of visuals of her battered body. "It's a good thing you didn't find her."

With a manicured nail, Eva swiped a tear from her cheek. "I was with her earlier that day, remember? That's how I prefer to remember her. We'd gotten coffee, and she couldn't stop talking about that Russian guy. You know the one." She waved a hand in the air.

"Yeah, but she was engaged to Tony." Em locked onto Eva,

and that sense of predatory stillness surrounded her. Em was badass.

"She was, yeah." Eva shrugged. "It was harmless. She didn't get together with him or anything." Her phone rang, and she dug through her purse for it. After peeking at the number, she hit Ignore then got to her feet. "I've got to run."

We returned the hugs as she went around the table. "It was great to catch up with you all. Let's pick a weekend to get away, yeah?"

"Definitely." Sofia gave her a small wave then turned back to Em and me. "Marissa never mentioned the Russian."

Ivan was a member of the Bratva—Russian Mafia. "I still think it was Tony." Every muscle tightened. I hated him. "He left campus around the time she died."

"The Russian is suspect by his demeanor alone. But I'm leaning toward Tony too." Emiliana then shared a conspiratorial look with Sofia. "We got you a little something for tonight."

I couldn't help the smile of anticipation as Sofia withdrew a long velvet box and handed it to me. After flipping the lid open, I lifted out a sapphire-tipped hairpin. So pretty. I would have to wear my hair in a bun then thread the long wooden stick through it tonight. "Since it's wood and not metal, how does it work as a weapon?"

An evil grin curved Em's glossy red lips. "Use your nail against the edge of the wood." She reached over, plucked it from my hand, then twisted her hair up. Shifting so her back was to me, she showed how the hairpin secured the mass in place then demonstrated with her right hand. Grasping the gemstone, she used the nail on her thumb to hold the small lip of the wood encasement in place while she pulled. Once the metal blade was clear, she didn't need to keep her thumb there, and it slid free easily.

"Be careful." Sofia's harsh whisper stopped me midreach. "It's razor-sharp and laced with truth serum. Trey said it's really concentrated."

Trey was Sofia's youngest brother and an off-the-charts genius. He was the doctor and surgeon to the five families. Giddy excitement over the new weapon caused a laugh to bubble up as Emiliana reattached the sheath then put the accessory back in the box.

"Tony pisses me off on the regular." I grinned. "He wouldn't be surprised if I sliced him with this."

"That's the plan." Emiliana snapped the lid shut with a resounding click. "If you can get him to confess to Marissa's murder—"

"Then we make him pay." We shared a look of determined retribution. The night of Marissa's death, Em, Sof, and I made a pact to be there for each other no matter what, no questions asked. I did not doubt that Tony had killed Marissa in a fit of rage, and soon, we would exact revenge.

CHAPTER SIX

MAX

After Liliana hugged her friends, I ushered her to the car with my hand on the small of her back. I liked seeing her with her guard down, relaxed and having fun with them. I opened the car door and waited for her to get in until rounding the front, constantly scanning our surroundings, then took a seat behind the wheel. I took a glance at the sky then closed the roof in case it rained.

The engine purred to life, and I pulled the car away from the curb, leaving Liliana's friends behind at the restaurant. Traffic was heavy, and clouds rolled in. There would be another storm that night, in more ways than one. As I shifted lanes and weaved through cars, the slight curve of her lips drew me, and I wanted to know what was on her mind.

I hadn't been far when she was with her friends and had caught enough of their conversation. The woman sitting in the passenger seat intrigued me. "What are you thinking?"

She started at my question then turned to face me. Large blue eyes met mine, but I had to refocus on the road so we didn't crash. Fat drops of rain hit the windshield, and I turned on the wipers, the swoosh of the blades the only sound between us. "Are you worried about the dinner tonight?" From my peripheral vision, I noted the slight tilt to her head at my question.

"Not really." She cleared her throat. "If I need you, whose side will you be on?"

"I'm your guard." *Or a glorified babysitter.* "Of course I'm on your side."

"That's not why my father brought you in, though. He'll change his mind on a dime. When you're no longer ordered to keep me safe, then what?"

I knew what she was asking. I'd been inside the house and felt the tension between her and Benito. "I'm always on your side." It was a partial truth. I wouldn't let anything happen to her. Her real threat was me. She just didn't know it.

"I can pay you. I know Benito does, but to make sure I'm safe, I can hire you. He'll never know. I have money."

"Just what do you think is going to happen tonight? That's what this is about, isn't it?" I wanted to take her hand in mine and reassure her that we were a team, even though that wasn't the case. But I would keep her safe. She had my word on that. No harm would come to her.

"You heard my father. I'm the key to his destiny. Whatever is going to hell in his business to cause him to make a deal with a cartel behind the family's back tells me just how desperate he is. So yeah, something is going to happen. If not tonight, then soon. He needs power. I'll be used to broker it."

Fuck it. I took her hand in mine for a brief squeeze, noting the flare of interest in her intense gaze. "Just like with the cartel scumbag spiking your drink, I've got your back. Trust me. And I don't need your money."

Everything in me stilled at the blinding smile that transformed her face from beautiful to stunning. I wanted her badly, and there was no sense in denying it. At the revelation, I mentally adjusted the trajectory of my plans for the possibility of her. "Tell me about Marissa. You were there the night she died?"

A flash of lightning split the sky, highlighting the flood of pain that engulfed her expressive eyes. "How do you know about her?"

I grimaced, trying to look guilty. "I moved forward when you lowered your voice and overheard you talking with your friends. No one else would have been able to hear. I was positioned where it was possible."

"Oh." She paused for a moment. "We were in college, soon to graduate. Marissa was newly engaged to Tony Caruso and not that happy about it. I can't say I blame her. Tony's not my favorite, and the thought of the Rossi family having ties to the Carusos? Yeah, that's probably not a good thing."

"The Rossi family has seen their fair share of tragedy. I can imagine that a wedding, and one that would bring greater stability within the five families, would be wanted."

"Have you met Frank Rossi?" He was the head of the Rossi family and Marissa's dad.

"From Sicily, remember?" I grinned at her. "I know of him but have yet to meet him face-to-face."

"Well, he's a monster. You aren't missing out. I'm not fond of Antonio Caruso, either. If either of them hires you in the future, keep that in mind."

A swift rush of anger momentarily blinded me as I imagined even the remotest interaction between Liliana and Antonio Caruso before I reined it in. I pulled off at the exit that would take us to the mansion where Liliana lived. Our secluded time together was coming to an end, and I wanted to learn more from her while she was being so open. "Tell me about the Russian and Tony."

"Wow. I didn't think we were that loud." She shook her head, her long blond hair shifting over her shoulders. "We'll have to be more careful in the future." Silence hung between us for a moment until she seemed to come to a conclusion. "If we're allies, then I trust that you'll keep anything I tell you in confidence."

She should have known better, but I had no reason to betray her. At least not in this. "We already established that."

She gave a small huff then opened up. "Tony is an entitled, power-hungry asshole. He's slightly older than Sofia, Emiliana, and me. He finished college the year before us, but we had to suffer his presence on campus for three years."

"He was engaged to Marissa?" I needed to keep her focused on who I wanted to know about the most, as we were minutes from her home. The trees alongside the road were old and huge, the houses spaced out for maximum privacy.

"Yeah. It was an arranged marriage, as I said earlier. Marissa wasn't as opposed to the idea as the rest of us would have been. Tony likes the clubs, and they hung out as friends, I guess. Even Eva, her best friend, thought it was a good match. But Eva's like that." She worried her bottom lip with her teeth for a moment. "Marissa was, too, actually. Tony had been seen on campus after Marissa was beaten then stabbed multiple times. I can't help to think that he had a hand in her death. What we've been struggling with is why."

"Tony's marriage to Marissa would have been a good move for him and his family. I'm not sure of the motive either."

"Well, there was one."

"And the Russian? Ivan, I think you called him?"

"Pretty sure he's Bratva." Russian Mafia. "The man was unapproachable, standoffish. With reason, of course. I mean— Italians surrounded him at the college. I have no idea why, but Marissa had her eye on him. Eva too. Tony's jealous and extremely possessive about anything he considers his, and something else has always been off about him." She pursed her lips. "Only-child syndrome."

I couldn't help but laugh at that.

"Yeah, I see the irony there, as I'm one too. In my defense, I wasn't spoiled like he was, and I had Sofia, Emiliana, and Marissa as sisters throughout my life. It's different. I swear."

"I'll take your word for it."

"No need. You'll see for yourself tonight."

I spotted the patrol as I swung into the driveway. The guard's intervals had a lag time that would be easy to exploit. Benito and his head of security weren't as skilled as they thought they were. Given the attack that had cost him his wife's life years before, he should have rectified that.

Instead of parking in the garage, I pulled around the circular driveway and stopped at the front door before shutting the engine off. Liliana looked at the door, and a soft sigh left her lips. It was evident that she didn't want to go in. My hand fisted, and I had to force myself to relax. A few more days, and everything would change. She just had to hold out.

I needed a reason to exploit the live-wire attraction between us, so I leaned over her to open her door, pausing with our faces inches apart. My gaze dropped to her lips then back up, causing her breath to go shallow. When her pupils dilated, I tried to remain unaffected, but it was damn hard. There was more I needed—wanted—from her.

Her lips parted, and I leaned in, brushing mine across hers. Something exploded between us. Her hands threaded through my hair, holding me in place. The world winked out as I explored her mouth, the soft moan at the back of her throat sending another wave of lust through me.

An alarm blared in my mind, and I slowed our kiss then pulled back. I was acting as her guard. We could not be together that way. Still, I didn't back away. Her eyes were glazed and passion-filled. Under her spell, despite my internal objections, I lost sight of the end goal for a split second. "If you could have anything in the world, what would you want?" *What the fuck was that?*

"A family," she whispered longingly.

"You have a family. A powerful one."

She shook her head. "This is a gilded prison. I want a real one that's full of love, not based on power, lies, and how often I can be useful, used."

I was going to hell. On that note, I opened her door then put needed space between us. As she got out, I watched her graceful walk, my body responding in ways I couldn't give in to. Her platinum hair hung down her back, almost to her waist, and drew my focus to the perfect curve of her ass then her long legs. There wasn't anything about her that didn't appeal to me.

I got out of the car, tossing the keys to one of the foot soldiers nearby, and followed Liliana inside. I didn't expect to feel so possessive. It complicated things, but only a little.

There were no shipments expected that night. Benito wanted things quiet so nothing would detract from his meeting with Antonio for reasons he would not disclose. Because of that, my presence wasn't necessary, but he granted my offer to watch over his daughter so long as I was on the outskirts of the meal, ensuring her safety after leaving the dining room. He must not have trusted Tony.

I hated Benito almost as much as she did, but for different reasons. My senses sharpened in anticipation of the upcoming dinner and my first encounter with the Caruso father and son. I would take from the Caruso family until Antonio had nothing left.

That night would be the beginning of the end.

CHAPTER SEVEN

LILIANA

I felt him on the other side of my bedroom door. I don't know how or why. Matt's presence sent a shiver of anticipation. *When I open it, will his eyes darken with desire as they sometimes do?*

I couldn't tell whether he would act on it or not. If it had been anyone else, I wouldn't have allowed even a hint of the attention he'd already shown me, subtle but so hot. For whatever reason, I craved his presence.

Only a handful of hours had passed since I was in the car with him. *And that kiss.* Already, I craved more. Matt had that effect on me.

I chose my outfit carefully, deciding on a black maxi dress with a plunging V-neck and a slit from ankle to midthigh. I had a knife strapped to my right thigh, hidden by the fabric's folds. Forgoing a necklace, I wore sapphire teardrop earrings and completed my accessories with my gifted hairpin. Slipping heels on, I opened the door then held still.

Matt leaned against the opposite wall but straightened when I stood before him. I took a step forward, closing the distance, and shut the door behind me. His gaze held me immobile, and I waited for him to say something.

"You look beautiful." His voice was deeper, guttural, as if it took an effort to get the words out. I understood.

Everything about him drew me in. The fact that he was seriously gorgeous and built was one thing, but most of the men at the top of the five families were, and I was used to being around guys who looked like models. It was the power that sizzled around him, and the offer of protection was the icing on the cake. He treated me as if I was important, worthy, and it melted my heart. "Thank you."

His palm settled on my lower back, and we made our way to the dining room. The touch sent jolts of awareness through my body, and his proximity caused my head to swim.

As we rounded a corner and entered the foyer, I caught a glimpse of us in a mirror and gasped at the image of us together. I shifted an inch closer. *What I wouldn't give for things to be different.* But he was a hitman, assumed to be a soldier by everyone who wasn't privy to his Sicilian pedigree. There would be no way my father would allow anything to come of whatever Matt and I had between us. And there was no denying there was something there.

We passed through two rooms until the heady scent of basil and garlic emanated from the dining room. The murmur of deep voices traveled just past the door, and I bit back a curse. They were early.

Matt's hand fell away, and he bent so he could whisper in my ear. "I'll be just outside the room if you need me. Come this way when you leave, and I'll make sure you get back to your room safely."

I nodded, schooling my features into a tranquil mask before I entered the dining room. *It shouldn't have to be this way. I should be safe in my own house. If Mom was alive, everything would be different.*

Sometimes, I tortured myself and thought about what could have been. It was a foolish game. I let the cold hard truth settle around me in a protective shield against what was to come. I stepped fully inside and met my father's furious gaze. Not for the first time, I noticed how we looked nothing alike. While his hair was dark, mine was light. Even our builds were opposite. I favored Mom's willowy frame.

I'd lined my eyes in smoky makeup, and as I tipped my chin down, keeping my eyes fixed on my father, I telegraphed how angry I was to be here. A flash of disdain pierced the arctic chill that emanated from him before he got control of his emotions. I bit back a smile. Victory surged, and I stood taller at having ruffled his feathers in the presence of his guests, though I hardly thought of any of the five families as such. Sometimes enemies and sometimes allies was more like it. Either way, we had to be on alert.

"And here is my errant daughter." My father waved his hand in my direction, ushering me to join him.

There was no way I could defy the gesture without causing harm to myself when no one was around. I crossed the room, only pausing by a waiter to pluck a glass of wine from the tray he held at the ready. After I had my drink, he made himself scarce, hurrying to the kitchen.

I skirted around the dining room table set with the finest crystal and china and stopped by my father's side. Facing Antonio Caruso, the head of the Caruso Italian-American Mafia family, and his son Tony, I plastered a smile on my face.

There was no mistaking how devastatingly handsome Antonio was, despite the slight gray at his temples and the scar above his eyebrows. It only made him appear distinguished, hiding the ugliness inside. Tony wasn't much better. His mean streak was always visible in his cold eyes. I'd been shoved off slides or tripped on the playground as a kid one too many times to ever take my eyes off him. Sofia took the brunt of it, for some reason. Marissa, he'd ignored more often than not. We'd been jealous of her for that.

"Each day, you grow to resemble your mother more." Antonio took my hand in his, pressing a kiss to the back of it.

I repressed a shudder at the unwanted brush of his too-wet lips. *Gross.* There was nothing I liked about the man. "Thank you. If only she were here."

"Hmm." His gray eyes narrowed a smidgen as his gaze bounced over my features. "If only."

Weird. What am I supposed to make of that? Tony cleared his throat, and I shifted my focus to him. Handsome and with a lean-but-strong physique, he was a carbon copy of his father, except for his shorter stature and softer features that resembled his mother, Nicole, who was noticeably absent.

"Liliana. It's been too long." Tony took my hand in his then pulled me in for a hug, brushing a kiss against my cheek.

"It has." My skin was on a constant crawl status from all the touching they were doing. I needed space. As soon as I could, I stepped back and away under the guise of searching the room for Antonio's wife. "Where's Nicole? Is she joining us tonight?"

"She should be here any moment. She stopped at the restroom on our way in," Antonio said.

I nodded. "That's great. Somehow, I missed seeing her a few months ago." I left that hanging, waiting to see if either of them picked up on the hint about Marissa's funeral, where Nicole had been noticeably absent.

"Liliana, dear, don't you look beautiful!"

Nicole's too-loud voice halted our conversation, and I turned as the cherub-faced blond made her way into the dining room. The woman liked to make a dramatic entrance where all eyes were on her, which she made possible largely with her sequined silver evening gown that made my plunging neckline seem modest. While mine hinted at what was beneath, she fairly spilled out of her dress. Not for the first time, I wondered if there was an inch of her the plastic surgeon she must have had on retainer hadn't touched.

Her hourglass figure—or Jessica Rabbit, rather—gave Eva a run for her money. I wanted to laugh at the few times I had been present to see Eva's narrowed gaze and veiled comments to Nicole. There was nothing fake on Eva, something that men openly appreciated. I knew from witnessing it far too often, growing up and at college. There was never a shortage of boyfriends.

I barely remembered what Nicole looked like when Antonio married her. I was pretty young, but so was she. She glided forward, accepted a kiss on the cheek from Antonio, then grasped my hands in front of her. "Stunning, Lil. What I wouldn't give to have that complexion or hair."

"We both have blond hair, Nicole." I barely stopped myself from rolling my eyes. It didn't matter.

Tony snorted, and an almost indiscernible flinch registered on Nicole. "I don't think that's even your real color, is it, Mom? Didn't you dye it lighter to match Elena's?" A sneer curved his mouth.

Antonio flicked his gaze over Nicole then turned to my dad in a dismissive manner that made my temper flare. "Why wouldn't she?" I shrugged. "She has the beauty to wear any color she wants and still look stunning." Before I said what I really wanted to, I looped my arm through Nicole's and pulled her to the side. Her presence gave me a reason to put more space between the men and us. I would get the answers I needed from Tony later. It wasn't the time. "Let's get you a glass of wine." *Or a bottle each.*

"Thanks," Nicole said, her usual upbeat energy noticeably dampened.

I flashed her a closed-lip smile. I couldn't exactly call him an ass. If I had been his mom, I would have dyed my hair the color of Elena's, too, to resemble her rather than him. Letting it go, I drew her away a few feet as a waiter entered the dining room with another glass on the tray, intended for Nicole. After she took her first sip, I waved him back and requested that a bottle be brought out. A single glass here and there wasn't going to cut it for either of us. Besides, Nicole drank heavily. My father couldn't chastise me here or later for indulging our "guest."

"What have you been up to?" We withdrew to two high-backed chairs in the corner of the room with a small end table between them. She looked like she would appreciate getting off her feet with those three-inch heels. She tried too hard to be closer to my age, even if she was a young mother to Tony.

"Shopping." Her smoker's voice purred. It worked for her. "What else is there? You know that's my addiction. Speaking of which, will you be going to Milan this year for the fashion shows?"

I motioned to the waiter, who hovered discreetly by the wall near my shoulder, to refill Nicole's glass, as she'd already polished it off. I'd managed half of mine and envied how she could drink with abandon. If I could've, I would've joined her. My gaze landed on Tony, who studied me in turn. Nope, I couldn't overindulge. I needed to be on top of my game.

"Milan." I addressed Nicole's question. "I might. Sofia will be there this year. She has a line that's being featured."

"That's right!" Nicole leaned forward and grabbed my forearm, squeezing it. "That settles it. I'm going. Antonio will have to arrange his schedule to make it happen." She looked at him from under her lashes, and they shared a silent communication that I didn't quite catch. "And we should make a point of getting together more often, just us girls."

I'd rather not. But maybe I should. Whatever that look was between her and Antonio, I didn't like the way they seemed to be conspiring about something. My back straightened, and I sucked in a breath. *Do they know what my dad is planning?*

Before I could question her, the waitstaff swooped in, and

we congregated at the table where they served dinner. The conversation centered on frivolous matters. Time passed much quicker than I thought it would. Before I knew it, the meal was over. Antonio and my father talked in hushed voices while a drunk Nicole leaned on her husband's arm to keep from falling off her chair and face-planting. Tony's gaze hadn't strayed from mine often, and with dinner over, he sought me out. Fine by me. It's what I wanted anyway.

We migrated from the table, and Nicole's grip remained on Antonio's arm, her balance precarious. I stood near the exit that was the most direct route to my room and away from that train wreck of an evening. The way Tony leered at me was different than before. It was almost possessive, which made no sense. There was no way in hell I would let him touch me. I had zero interest in him.

Eva thought he was attractive. I did not. But it didn't matter what I thought. I had to suck it up and get him to think I was at least a little interested so he would go off with me for a few minutes.

I pivoted from my position by the table so that my back was to him. Swaying my hips enough for him to notice, I took a few steps in the direction of the hallway that led to the foyer, pausing to look over my shoulder in invitation. His eyes flared, and he moved forward, taking the bait. The corridor was dimly lit, and as I passed by Matt, electricity pulsed over every inch of me, making the tiny hairs at my nape stand at attention.

With a slight shake of my head, I tried to convey that I didn't want him to stop Tony from following. It didn't take long before Tony's hand closed around my arm. We were close to the foyer's marble tiles, and with a slight urging, I got him into the open area with better lighting. I wanted to be able to see every expression that crossed his face when I asked my questions.

"Why is it that we never went out?" Tony's brows rose,

somehow making his round face even more boyish. The expression reminded me of his mother.

"Why?" I twisted out of his hold then smoothed the lapel of his jacket to dispel the perceived rejection. "You were with Marissa." I reached up, my fingers grasping the sapphire hairpin and pulling it out. I shook my head, letting the long strands tumble down my back. He watched with abject fascination. "I'm sure you were devastated by her loss."

"It's early! Let's go to Envy." Nicole's slightly slurred voice bounced off the walls.

I wanted to scream. The hairpin was in my hand and positioned where I wanted it. If Tony made a move, I would have been able to accidentally slice his hand as I pretended to reach for him.

Tony didn't pay any attention to our party growing from two to five. "Marissa. Of course, such a loss."

"It was a shame that she died. That college was supposed to have top-notch security," Antonio snapped. "As it should have, since we own it."

"We do?" Nicole clung to him, tilting her head as she asked her question. She teetered back, and Antonio slipped his arm around her waist to hold her to him.

"It's Mafia owned." Antonio seemed to hedge a bit.

My father interjected. "And the only reason I allowed Liliana to attend."

"By us?" Nicole was like a dog with a bone. She pushed, and Antonio's face turned red, anger sparking at her insistence.

"Frank Rossi."

"Oh." She hiccupped, her eyelids dropping to half-mast. "Too bad she died, then. We would have had a piece of that."

"The connection would have been beneficial," Antonio said from between clenched teeth. "It's a shame they didn't have another available daughter."

"Frank isn't the only one with connections," my father interjected.

That was strange. I shifted my focus from Tony to my father.

"What is this, now?" Nicole's head swung to Benito, and Antonio had to adjust her again so she didn't fall, his annoyance at her antics clear in way a muscle jumped along his jaw.

"Take your mother to the car, Tony," he snapped.

Tony opened his mouth to protest. Antonio growled, and that was the end of it.

The evening wrapped up quickly after Tony and Nicole were out the door. I lingered on the edge of the conversation until my father leveled me with a glare. That was my cue. I exchanged goodbyes with Antonio, saying that I would call and check on Nicole in the morning.

As I exited the foyer and entered the hall, my steps slowed until I was just out of sight but still close enough to overhear a few words. I shivered, not from cold, but from Matt's proximity as he joined me. Without thought, I leaned into him, needing his heat and that ever-present sense of security I felt when around him. The front door opened, and I strained to hear what else was said.

"With the distrust between the families and the war coming—"

Maybe I shouldn't have eavesdropped because my father's words sent a wave of fear through me, resurrecting nightmares I fought to keep buried.

CHAPTER EIGHT

LILIANA

Since the dinner the night before, I'd been nothing but preoccupied. In the early morning hours, my reoccurring nightmare had attempted to sink its talons deep into me, but I had been aware enough to jerk awake and push it away.

Unlike the day before, the sun shone without a cloud in the sky. I sat up in bed, the covers pooling around my waist, then grabbed my phone to conference with Sofia and Emiliana. We needed to reconvene and plot our next move.

"Girl," Em growled. "You better have an I-got-a-confession-from-Tony reason to call this early in the morning."

Sofia's sleepy "'lo" right after made me smile despite the dismal news I had for them.

"No. Nothing much came of the evening." I rubbed my forehead, feeling a headache coming on. "I was only alone with him for a few minutes."

"So no hairpin stabbing?" Em asked.

"I had it in my hand, ready to cut and infect him with the truth serum, but then my father and Antonio interrupted with a very tipsy Nicole."

"There'll be another opportunity," Sofia said, ever the optimist.

"Tell us about the dinner." Em sounded more awake.

"It was creepy, as expected. Honestly, I'm more confused about Antonio's intentions for Tony than ever. Other than that, I'm more sure that Tony murdered Marissa. They were friends at the very least, and she was to become his wife. There was *no* remorse over her death. He's guilty, has to be."

"We all think it." Sofia's words elongated on a yawn that she smothered. "We saw his hands at the funeral, the bruised and scabbed knuckles."

"That says something," Em agreed. "We should have found a way to get him to confess there and then ended him."

"It was unfortunate that all those people were in the way and not enough evidence. We would have had the entire Mafia on our backs. We weren't ready. I am now."

"Same," both Em and Sofia agreed.

We let the silence stretch for a moment, each of us lost in thought. "Sof, I know your fashion show is in a couple of weeks and you're crazy busy getting ready, but do you guys think we could meet for coffee?" I needed some isolated time with the two of them before dealing with all those reporters and cameras that were inevitable at the event.

"Of course," Sofia said warmly.

"What time?" The sound of the shower starting came through Em's receiver.

"An hour." I glanced at the time. "I'll see you soon. I've to get in the shower too."

"Are you sure everything is okay? You seem a little off," Sofia said.

"I'm all right. It's just that I have a bad feeling everything's about to change."

We got off the phone, and I hurried into the shower. After washing my hair, I blow-dried it and left it hanging down my back in long loose waves. With one last swipe of the brush, and I exited my en suite with a towel wrapped around my body.

Mentally, I sifted through what I wanted to wear when I opened the door to pass through my room to the closet. Awareness crackled in the air, and I froze. Something was off. *Had I locked my bedroom door?*

Then I felt him. My gaze darted around my room, and I tried to dispel the vulnerability of my situation. I had no weapon and wore only a towel.

Matt cleared his throat. "I knocked, but I don't think you heard me over the hairdryer."

He leaned one broad shoulder against the doorframe. *So tall and devastatingly handsome.* I wished I wasn't Benito's daughter and that I could lose myself in Matt's gray eyes. It wasn't hard to imagine how he would touch me. My blood heated. I wanted him. All it would take was loosening my towel, and by the way his pupils were dilated and his skin stretched tightly across his features, I had no doubt he'd follow through how I wanted him to.

"I'm not going to be around today," he said.

I jerked, my cheeks flushing from the trajectory of my thoughts. Then he broke eye contact, and I forced myself to stop overthinking things. I was being ridiculous. "That's fine."

"Had I known you would be getting out of the shower"—a corner of his mouth lifted in a sexy smirk—"I still would have come in. Worth it."

A laugh burst free, dispelling my insecurities. I felt lighter than I had since the day before at lunch. That reminded me that I had to get going if I wanted to be on time. "That's fine. I'm going to meet with my friends for coffee."

His body tensed as if he didn't like my plans. I crossed my arms beneath my breasts, and his gaze skimmed the top of the towel. Fighting a grin, I held still until his face was stoic and his muscles relaxed again. *What would it be like if he acted on the attraction between us? If I had more time, I might push him.*

"Take Vinnie. He's the most reliable and skilled of Benito's soldiers." With a "be careful," he was out the door, the click of it providing the only evidence that he was there.

I stood still for another moment, pursing my lips and contemplating what hadn't happened. With another glance at the clock, I marched over to the door, threw home the lock, then went into my closet. I plucked a white bell-sleeved silk blouse from the rack along with a black leather miniskirt and my favorite red-soled Louboutins. I ran my fingers over the jewelry box that held the hairpin. If it had gone with my outfit, I would have worn it. Instead, I strapped a knife to the inside of my forearm, hidden by the length of my sleeve.

I might not have needed the blade, but it was foolish to go anywhere without a weapon. Good thing I was meeting the girls. I gave the hairpin one last glance but doubted I would encounter Tony. I tossed the towel into the hamper, grabbed my clutch, then exited my room. Out of habit, I took the route past my father's office. It was foolish, but any information I could overhear helped me remain on top of things and stay the hell out of my father's way and whatever his plan was.

I popped open my clutch to double-check that my gun was in there and to add my cell. The thin belt I wore had a small choke wire hidden inside. My altered and weaponized vintage two-toned diamond Rolex watch contained another wire that Sofia's brother had added. I didn't know what we would do without Sofia's brothers. Enzo was fiercely protective of his sister, Emiliana, but lately, he didn't hang around Sofia and me as much as he used to. We hadn't been able to figure out what was going on with him. Em's family was great, but I loved Sofia's as if they were my own. I wished they were.

Wherever the three of us went, we weaponed up. That was a cardinal rule of the Mafia. Guards died, and we had to be able to protect ourselves. My father hadn't equipped me with the skills to fight or shoot a gun, but Sofia's brothers had. I was eternally grateful to them.

The click of my heels couldn't be helped against the hallway's wood floors as I neared my father's office. It was nine and early for him to have a meeting, but the faint murmur of men's voices drifted toward where I listened. It took a moment before I recognized who my father had in there. Antonio. *This can't be good.*

I inched forward on the balls of my feet, careful to keep any noise from my heels to a minimum. Hand trailing the wall, I paused when I got within a foot of the open door.

My heart pounded against my rib cage. If my father caught me, I wouldn't be going anywhere. His punishment for eavesdropping was locking me in my room for a day or two with no food or access to anyone in the house. He would station guards at my door twenty-four seven to enforce his order until he decided to let me rejoin the household, beginning with a lecture about how lacking I was as a daughter. He would also tack on how worthless I was with not even a fraction of my mother's beauty and charm.

That was not something I wanted to repeat anytime soon, especially as I had an agenda with Tony. And the thought of being separated from Matt, the only guard I'd grown attached to, didn't sit right.

What my father didn't know was that I had an escape, thanks to my friends and a lot of YouTube instructions. There were days when my father wasn't at home, and that's when Em and Sof and I had made modifications to my room—with music blasting, of course. We couldn't have his soldiers privy to what we were doing.

When Sofia and Emiliana had learned about what he would do, they were determined to help, and under the pretense of a sleepover the summer after our freshman year in college, they brought tools over in a suitcase. It wasn't hard. My parents had a hidden room off their closet. Mine was still in the same wing as theirs. We cut out the wall behind a bookcase, added invisible hinges, then disguised the outside so it was impossible to tell it swung inward. I had access to the secure room that my father would never use. It had been made for my mother and a space he chose to forget.

The three of us were the only ones who knew about it. I could sneak out in the early morning hours, as that's when most of the household was asleep and there were very few soldiers to encounter. I'd gotten better at spying and so far had only had to use it one time. Since then, I'd stocked snacks inside, a burner phone if I couldn't get to mine before going in, and water. I had a spare gun in the rafters, where there was a shelf big enough to hold me. People rarely looked up. It's what I would rely on if my father remembered the room.

Snapping back to the present and the increased volume of Antonio's voice, I checked my watch. It was getting late. I had to get out of there if I was going to meet Sofia and Emiliana on time, and the men's loud voices made me worry that they were on their feet and near the door. I had to pass it before they spotted me. Shifting to the other side of the wall, I made sure to let the sound of my heels be heard as I moved forward at a brisk pace.

At the open door, I faltered for some unknown reason. Maybe it was the tone Antonio used when he said, "You have nothing to offer."

Both men were on their feet. My heart stuttered a beat, and I sucked in a breath as I turned, catching my dad's eye as he stood behind his oversized mahogany desk. "But I do. You have an unmarried son."

I froze. *What the hell is he doing? Why would he even consider Tony?* One look, and he'd conveyed I was to remain. My body trembled. The premonition from that morning about how everything would change was blaring like a siren through my head, slashing my soul to bloody ribbons.

Antonio's head turned, and a spark of interest shone in his calculating brown eyes. *Holy shit.* I was in the sniper's sight with those two. My body refused to obey my order to flee. It wouldn't have mattered if I had. Dad would have ordered his soldiers to detain me by whatever means necessary.

"My business will expand once I absorb the cartel's operation in our city. There is only one way to get in on it." My father dangled the carrot.

"I believe we have a deal."

"I took the liberty of having my lawyers draw up a contract." My father placed papers in front of Antonio, who returned to the desk. He lifted them and read.

The minutes ticked by with agonizing slowness. I didn't dare move. I needed to hear whatever would come from the conversation, and my father would humiliate me if I left before he dismissed me.

After Antonio finished reading the last page, he shook my father's hand. "Everything is in order, then." With a scrawl of their signatures on two copies of the agreement, they concluded their meeting.

Antonio checked his watch. "I have another appointment. We'll be in touch." He left the office without a word to me. Another moment passed as both my father and I watched Antonio's retreating form. Then my father grabbed my elbow and pulled me inside his domain. The door shut behind me with an ominous click.

I trembled as he dropped the document in front of me. I scanned it with dawning horror. I'd heard what they were negotiating, but to see it in writing and signed was another thing entirely.

The words: bound by Mafia code, arranged marriage between Antonio Caruso's eldest son and Benito Brambilla's daughter. I read the main points in the contract: will protect, physically and financially, blah blah blah, an alliance between the two families, blah blah. What stood out, though, was "failure to comply by either party will result in an active declaration of war." *Holy hell.* He'd signed my future away to someone who repulsed me on the regular.

The fight with the Espinosa cartel for territory and control would be a bloody one, which was why he needed Antonio's money and his army. That had to have been the war he kept referencing. I was simply the bartering chip to get what he wanted.

My father yanked the paper back, so I couldn't tear it to shreds. I lifted my hate-filled gaze from the desk to his, fury boiling in my veins.

"Liliana. You will not leave the premises." With a gleeful expression carved onto his evil face. "War is coming, and you will be my sacrifice."

CHAPTER NINE

LILIANA

My hands shook as I raced down the hallway toward my room while my dad barked orders to the three soldiers he'd summoned. I was on lockdown, as Benito knew I was a flight risk. I was done referring to him as my father, at least in my thoughts. I wasn't stupid enough to call him that to his face.

I wondered if the war he was referencing would only be with the cartel or if it would also include Frank Rossi, and that was why he needed Antonio Caruso. Rossi's was the only arm of the five families that made sense. He was equally cruel and dangerous. Benito hated him with a passion. I knew he thought Frank was responsible for Mom's death, but he wasn't able to prove it.

Once inside my room, I slammed the door and slid the bolt home. It wouldn't stop them from getting in, but it would give me time. In my closet, I stripped out of my clothes and replaced them with the form-fitting black pants and tight black Henley that Sofia had made. With the bit of time I estimated as safe, I grabbed every weapon I had. Next, I took my phone and slipped it into a Faraday case then into a backpack, where the weapons also went.

Mom's diamonds were next. No way would I leave something that had such sentimental value to both of us. In a moment of weakness where I couldn't focus on the ticking clock, I let my hand trail over the case of charcoal pencils and the sketchpads beneath. One was mine, the other the last one Mom had worked in. With care, I put the items that mattered the most to me in the bag. They represented a snapshot in time of treasured memories with her.

I dropped to my knees and pulled out the bottom jewelry drawer. I had money underneath the velvet panel. The necklaces I kept on top weren't worth anything, but I lifted it with care so no one would think I'd stashed anything beneath it. Better to keep them thinking I was helpless instead of prepared and resourceful.

I grabbed stacks of hundreds and shoved them into my bag. After replacing the insert, I systematically went through the drawers and took every expensive watch, ring, bracelet, and necklace that I owned. If I was going off on my own—and I was —I would need money, as Benito would freeze my accounts, and those would sell well. Plus, I'd been putting off getting identification with a fake name. It was an oversight on my part but not something I couldn't rectify. Emiliana had contacts who were discreet and unknown by the Mafia, along with a plan in case things got too bad for her as well. Her father wasn't a monster like mine, but she'd been subject to mine long enough that he'd left a lasting impression.

My hands shook so badly that it took me several attempts to zip the bag closed. I went to the window and loosened the gauzy curtains so they hung down and obscured as much of the view of the room as possible. I should have gotten the blackout blinds installed that Emiliana suggested, but I thought my setup would be fine. What I hadn't considered was that Benito's soldiers could watch me from somewhere outside. If so, they would report that I'd never left my room.

Forcing myself to let that thought go, I kept moving. I would work with what I had. Once the curtains were in place, I shoved open the window then pushed the screen out so that it fell to the ground two stories below. It would be found, but that was the plan. Not far from my window was a thick tree branch. I knew it would be suicide to attempt the jump, but Benito would only think of how desperate I was and the hateful words I'd shouted as I ran from his office.

With the false trail in place, I skirted out of sight and raced to the hidden door behind the bookcase. Carefully, I swung it open then slipped inside, making sure it was closed securely behind me. Not an ounce of light penetrated the secret room. I bent and felt around on the bench seat that lined the opposite side of my bedroom wall, where I could lift the lid and store things. A penlight was where I'd left it in the crevice between the seat and wall. I had others stashed throughout the space if I needed them.

A beam of LED light shone on the unfinished plank floor with a click of the button on the small device. The room was sparse. I had a few books, a travel-sized pillow and blanket, and snacks in storage. That was about it, aside from my spare gun and phone charger.

I took my backpack off and withdrew a burner phone, leaving mine in the Faraday case so it couldn't send or receive a signal, then replaced the leather bag on my back. The straps were tight enough that it wouldn't hang down or swing and knock into anything or get in the way of what I might need to do.

I made sure the phone was on silent. I shot off texts to Sofia and Emiliana that I couldn't make it and that I was on lockdown.

Emiliana: *WHAT HAPPENED???*
Sofia: *YOU OKAY?*

Me: *I'm safe. In the secret room. Benito/Antonio signed a contract. Arranged marriage to Tony/me.*

Emiliana: *Shit! Wait—you'll be alone w/him.*

Sofia: *Not ideal. But Em's right.*

Me: *I can't marry him.*

Emiliana: *Not what we're suggesting. Get close/alone. Use the hairpin. Or I could?*

Me: *I have a better shot of getting close to him. He doesn't trust you.*

Sofia: **snorts coffee*

Emiliana: *Shut it.*

Me: *NOT marrying him.*

Sofia: *Don't want you to. Remember how Marissa died? It was done in rage.*

Emiliana: *I'll get to him before he can go near you. Stay hidden. Maybe Stefano can help. He wants revenge for his sister's murder.*

Me: *NO!!! Tell no one. Sof—promise.*

Sofia: *Why?*

Me: *We need a plan, and Benito is on a rampage. It's not safe to leave my spot. Will text later.*

Sofia: *Love you. Be safe.*

Emiliana: *Same. We got your back. Text us and we'll come running.*

I pushed out a breath then slid the burner phone into another Faraday sleeve before putting it in my back pocket. I pulled a book, book light, and a dark-blue fleece blanket from where it lay, folded inside the bench compartment, then spread it out on the long seat and stretched out on my stomach.

An hour passed before I heard the commotion below. I chuckled under my breath. They'd found the screen. Soon, they would be in my room, searching. That bothered me to no end, but it couldn't be helped. Not much in there was important aside from the pictures of my mom, but I'd taken that into account and made digital copies. They were safe, secure, and easy to reprint.

With the alarm raised and enough time having passed where they would do another search inside, it was time to camouflage myself further. I stowed the blanket back in the bench seat, the book underneath it, then dropped a false bottom over that for safe measure. No reason to let them know I'd been in here in the last few years by them finding a current bestseller, especially since Benito wouldn't think the room had been used after Mom died.

With the light guiding my way, I went to the back of the room, where there was a small black safe, entered the code, and withdrew documents and old pictures. With them in hand, I closed the metal door then stowed everything in my bag. There wouldn't be another opportunity to retrieve those documents once I was gone.

My fingers trailed across the wood floor at my knees. There was a reason I wasn't supposed to know about the secret room.

I gasped as images from the night Mom was murdered invaded my mind. Terror clawed at my throat. Tears sprung to my eyes before I had a chance to stop them.

I took slow breaths, focusing on gratitude. Mom had told me about it the night she'd died. Dad had made sure it was a secret. While they'd renovated the kitchen, another crew had created the room that sat hidden between theirs and mine. After, he'd killed them himself. There were no witnesses aside from my mom, whom he loved enough to risk the wrath of the Sicilians, should they find out what he'd done in order to win her.

He didn't know I'd found it. The documents. The pictures.

When I'd snooped in the room Mom had lost her life to take me to, I'd found the safe. The combination was easy to crack—the date he and Mom met. She'd told me about that day many times. A part of me wondered if she'd thought I would someday need insurance. Because that's what the information in the safe was: fodder for blackmail. With it, I was untouchable to Benito.

She'd armed me with the very thing that would stop him from coming after me. I only had to confront him. So far, I'd been afraid. Given the opportunity, he would kill me. No one in the house would have my back, except maybe Matt.

I held the penlight between my teeth then climbed onto the bench. The next part was a bit trickier. The edge of the steel beam at the top of the ceiling was a good two feet away. I bent my knees, swung my arms down, then jumped on the upswing. My fingers curled around the edge of the metal. Tightening my core, I swung a leg onto the ledge then struggled to pull myself up. It took a minute or two. By the time I was flat on the wide metal ledge, perspiration had coated my forehead and upper lip.

I swiped my face with a hand then tucked myself as far back as the narrow foot and a half-metal ledge allowed. *Shit. I forgot the black stocking.* It was still in my bag. No matter how dark it was in there, my hair was a beacon. If they shone any light up there, I would be spotted. Good thing I was hidden from the door he would access, facing mine instead. If I got lucky enough that Benito didn't walk all the way in and look up, I'd put it on when he left and keep it there.

About fifteen minutes passed before my father bellowed for someone to break down the door to my bedroom. A loud crash followed shortly after. I cringed at the sound of the splintering wood. They were inside my room. I clenched my teeth at the injustice of it. The day couldn't have gotten any worse.

My muscles tensed as I remained immobile, and I strained my ears to hear every word I could.

"Goddammit, Liliana!" Something crashed. Benito bellowed again. "Who the hell was patrolling the grounds?"

The response was too soft for me to hear, followed by another crash from what sounded like the window slamming shut.

"Bring those idiots to me. Have them wait in the hall by my office." Their voices faded. "I'll deal with them soon. Keep searching for her."

A chorus of doors slammed throughout the house as they looked everywhere on the off chance I was hiding inside the house. *Do they think I'm a child?* I couldn't help a grin from curving my lips. The irony wasn't lost. I was hiding.

Forty-five minutes later, the secret door in my parents' closet opened. Heavy footfalls, then a light shone around the bare space. A cramp seized my right calf, but I didn't dare shift while Benito was inside.

He crossed the room, and I could see the top of his head. A flick of his wrist, and he had the bench seat open. He cursed and let the lid slip from his hand, and it slammed home.

Good thing he only glanced around and hadn't noticed the false bottom.

"You're finally worth something, and now I can't find you. When I do, I promise you'll wish you had died that night." Benito cursed again before storming out of the cramped space, shutting the door and throwing the room back into inky darkness.

Pain pierced my heart. I hated him, but it didn't stop a part of me from craving his love. *How could he do this to me?*

If he'd had any love for me, it died the night my mother was murdered. He'd cursed me for taking her life. I hadn't, but Mom had thrown herself in front of me and taken the bullet that was meant for me. He never let me forget what a liability I was and how I'd cost him everything.

I angrily swiped at a tear. He wasn't worth it.

After another few minutes passed, and the door remained closed, I stretched out my calf by pulling my toes toward me. I didn't dare get down from my perch, even for the stocking cap. He could come back. It wasn't a chance I would risk after hearing his threat.

If I could have stayed in there until Antonio learned I was missing, there was a possibility he would hold Benito responsible. Especially if I didn't show before the wedding.

Hours passed. Dinner came and went. I ate a granola bar and washed it down with a few sips of water. It'd been a risk to come down from the beam, but I'd only done so for five minutes because I couldn't take my backpack off easily. It was enough time to secure my hair under the stocking cap. Then I'd hoisted myself back up onto the beam and settled in. There was no way I would leave the room until I was sure everyone was asleep. Even then, I couldn't cross the grounds until they all thought I'd left on foot and didn't suspect I was somewhere in the estate.

Voices leaked through the wall, and I stiffened. One was my father, but the other was too low for me to hear the words. Again, I strained my ears to hear everything I could. Knowledge was power, and I needed all that I could get.

One thing was clear. Benito was furious, and it wasn't the same as how he'd reacted to finding out that I was gone. He was livid. Anger like that in him usually resulted in casualties of anyone within firing range.

"What the hell are you talking about? And who the fuck are you?"

The other man was speaking, and I almost fell off the beam trying to hear what he said, catching myself at the last minute. Benito parroted parts of the conversation but not enough to make sense: "An indication of the type of businessman I am? You're begging me to kill you right here and now."

My mind whirled at the odd turn of events. Their voices faded, but I couldn't stop my thoughts from spinning. *Who else had been in my room? Was it Tony?*

The other man's menacing words weren't clear enough except for: "You have twenty-four hours to deliver her."

CHAPTER TEN

MAX

I did another sweep of the grounds on Liliana's side of the house while wearing night vision goggles. Benito's bedroom was also on the north side of the manor, and the light had gone out an hour before. A majority of the household was fast asleep, which meant it was our time to break in and do our surveillance.

A light breeze rustled the leaves of the tree where I was perched. It was the best view of her room, and I had a sense she was somewhere inside. Aside from the all-season room, her bedroom was the other place where she spent time. She only passed through the rest of the house, never stopping anywhere for more than a few minutes. My cousins hadn't reported that she'd left the house after the meeting or at all. She had to have been inside unless there was an escape tunnel.

In all black, none of us were likely to be spotted. Even Benito's soldiers patrolling below hadn't ID'd my cousins or looked up to where I was stationed in the tree.

"Report," I spoke in a hushed tone into the communication device on my wrist that my Sicilian cousins Tommasso, Salvio, and Cristiano shared. Sal, who monitored the front of the manor, was the first to respond.

"Everything is the same as an hour ago. No new guards have entered, and no sign of Liliana." The message from Sal came through my earpiece.

"Back of the house is quiet," Cristiano responded.

"Same on the south side. Soldiers walking the perimeter here have a long lag time, easy to infiltrate," Tommasso said.

We had a narrow window of time to break in and search. Tommasso and I would be the only two going in. "One minute." I gave the countdown for when he should enter as I swept the binoculars back to Lil's room.

Sixty seconds later, Tommasso reported the alarm was disabled and that he was in.

I was about to descend the tree when movement in Lil's room caught my eye. A small beam of light shone from the west wall in her room. The only thing I remembered along that side was a bookcase. I couldn't help my low chuckle. She must have had a secret room. How Benito hadn't found her was beyond me unless he didn't know about it, but that was impossible. The most likely scenario was that he was in on hiding her.

The light bobbed then disappeared where her bathroom should have been. I had minutes to get inside and into her room. As soon as one of the patrols walked by, I shimmied down the tree, jumping the last five feet to land in a crouch. My gun was in my hand instantly. When no alarm sounded, I led with my 9mm to one of the windows I'd unlocked when I was in the house last.

With barely a sound, I pushed the window up and climbed into the empty study. Books lined the walls, the shelves reaching to the ceiling. I couldn't imagine Benito as a reader. It must have been his late wife's or possibly Liliana's. Aside from the laundry room, I'd thought it would be the best place to enter and least likely to be checked for an unlocked window.

The night vision goggles were still in place, and I was able to make my way through the dark house without the aid of a flashlight. Slipping from the study, I hurried to the back stairs that would take me to Liliana's room. Two and a half minutes had passed, and I worried she would emerge from the bathroom before I could get into position.

The stairs were another issue altogether. When I worked in the home, I'd paid attention to which steps squeaked and where. Counting as I ascended, I placed my feet where they wouldn't make any noise. At the top of the landing, I increased my pace to her room.

The door was ajar, the wood around the lock and door handle splintered and littering the floor. I slipped off the goggles, as there was a sliver of light beneath the bathroom door. While she was inside, I crossed to the bookcase where it appeared she had come from. I ran my left hand over the sides of the small frame of the bookcase but couldn't find a button or lever to depress.

A toilet flushed, and I moved to the other side of her bed, lying flat on the floor. Water ran as she washed her hands, then the door opened. A thin beam of light bobbed and swept over the room in a hurried circle. As soon as the light dimmed and I knew she would have her back to me, I shifted to look around the side of the bed.

She wore tight-fitting black clothes that highlighted every line of her body. A black leather backpack was strapped against her back. A stocking cap covered her blond hair. I wanted to grab her and pull her against me then and there, but curiosity held me in place. Seeing what she did next would give me greater insight into how her mind worked.

On the third shelf from the top, she flipped a book on its side. The door didn't immediately open. She must have done something else. The point was that book was key to hiding the way to open the door. When she placed her hand on the base of the shelf and pushed, the bookcase swung inward. Not a sound was made. She stepped in and returned the door to its original position. I grinned. The seal was seamless and undetectable unless someone knew it was there.

I waited for two seconds then went to where she'd stood. Flipping the book on its side, I found what looked like a natural wood knot. Pushing on the dark center a soft click sounded, I returned the book to its position, and then I was able to move the door. Opening it just enough to slide in, I entered and carefully shut the door. If there was any way to keep my presence hidden from her for a few minutes, the better.

My back was to the closed door, and I spotted Liliana immediately. Penlight held between her lips, she dangled from a large support girder at the top of the ceiling. Her back was to me as she swung a leg up onto the beam then pulled herself the rest of the way up.

I held still, waiting to see what she did next before I made my presence known. There were some scuffling noises then a small flare of light that was probably from a phone.

"It's me." Lil's voice was hushed as she held a phone to her ear.

I was glad I waited. I needed to know what she planned, who was on the other end of the line. *Possibly her two friends? Or would she call Tony or another man?* A surge of unwanted jealousy flooded me.

"I'm okay. They haven't found me, but I think it's a good idea to get out of here tomorrow night about this time."

She fell silent as the other person responded, and I held myself rigid. My fingers twitched. I wanted to pull her off the beam and crush her phone.

"Who do you think would be safer to help me while keeping my secret? Marco, Enzo, or possibly even Stefano? What did Em say?"

I needed to check in with Stefano, the only underboss of the five families that I considered a friend of sorts. His life was equally fucked up, and we could commiserate. He didn't know I was back. It was probably time to update him.

"Okay, then. Thanks, Sof. I owe you and Enzo. Same time tomorrow. I'll be ready. Edge of the property, north side by that tree we used to climb when we were little."

A few seconds passed after she hung up. It was time to let her know I was there. Not wanting to scare her, I secured my gun in my waistband. I crossed to where she could see me from her position on the beam. "Lil. It's me," I whispered.

She jerked and her penlight fell. It never hit the floor. I caught it and pointed it down. Enough light was cast to see her shadowy form. She didn't utter a word, which told me she thought I'd switched to Benito's side and not hers.

"I'm here to get you out." I kept my voice soft. "You're safe. I'm not here on Benito's behalf."

She peeked over the edge of the beam. I lifted the light a little higher so I could make out her expression. Even in the dim lighting, I could see worry etched around her mouth. Her lips were pressed into a tight line, and she didn't say anything. I waited for her to come to a decision. Either way, she would be leaving with me, but it would be a hell of a lot easier with her as a willing participant. I'd rather not put duct tape on her, but I would do what I needed to.

"You shaved." Her eyes widened, and she scrutinized my face.

"Summer. It'll be hot with a beard. We can talk later. We need to leave."

"Where would you take me?"

"To my house. Benito would never think to look there. He doesn't know about it, and he wouldn't be able to gain entrance if he eventually found out."

"I can't stay there."

"You can't stay here."

"Why are you helping me?" She remained motionless.

I grinned, forcing myself to relax despite the urge to yank her from her post and drag her from the house. She was mine. She just didn't know it yet. I was never letting her go. "I thought we were friends, that we'd determined we're allies."

"I won't go back."

I raised my eyebrows, needing to clarify what "back" was to her. "To Benito?"

"Yes. I'm done. I know there's no way out of the Mafia, but I want out of *this* life."

"The way out from under your father's control is with me." It took everything in me to remain patient. "But you're right. You're Mafia. From that, you can never leave."

"You'll be taking me from one prison to another. How will that help me?" Her chin jutted out, stubbornness clear in her expression. "I should go with my plan. I have a better chance of making it out alive."

She didn't even know how right she was with that statement. "Haven't I looked out for you?"

"So far, yes. But you haven't been here long. You don't know what goes on."

"Trust me. My way, you'll still be able to see your friends." *Under my supervision,* but there was no way I would tell her that. "We've already spent too much time talking. The shift will change soon, doubling the guards on the grounds." At least until the ones relieved left, but I didn't want to take any chances of getting caught. "We need to go."

Another few seconds passed before she gave me a brief nod. Swinging her legs over, she positioned her hands on the edge of the support beam so she could drop. I gripped her waist then lifted her the rest of the way down. For a brief moment, I pulled her against me. The way her body molded to mine burned into my psyche. Her swift intake told me she, too, was affected.

I wanted her, but willingly. And what I wanted, I would have.

She turned in my arms, her gaze sweeping over what I was wearing then to the night vision goggles hanging around my neck.

"No." Her voice hardened, and she tried to pull back. "I'm not going anywhere with you. For all I know, you're a plant, working with the feds. I'm not a rat."

I underestimated her reaction. Her logic was sound. The enemy that she didn't know was probably worse than the one she'd lived with her entire life.

She would have been correct. I was so much worse. But not to her. Never to her.

She shoved at my chest, but it made no difference. "I'm not working with the feds." It didn't matter what I said. The way I'd found her, how I was dressed, the time of night… it all clicked. I could read it clearly on her face.

"But you aren't who you say you are. If you were, you would have found me during the day if you were able to. This"—she spread her fingers wide on my chest—"says differently. I trusted you." Her voice broke.

There was no helping for it. I grabbed her wrists, twisted them behind her back, and held them with one hand. With the other, I withdrew a zip tie from my pocket, slipped it around her wrists, then pulled the plastic strap tight. I bent to her ear and whispered, "This is just so you'll stop fighting me. We need to go." I grinned, letting my lips graze her ear. "You can tie me up later."

She shivered, and I took advantage, tossing her over my shoulder so I could move quickly and get us out of a potentially dangerous situation. When she wiggled, I slapped her butt, never expecting the curses to roll out of her mouth at the speed and volume that they did. I had to do something immediately, or we would be found out.

CHAPTER ELEVEN

LILIANA

The momentary shock from Matt smacking my ass didn't last long. His hand lingered past the sting and heat settled into places I wasn't ready to admit I wanted him to touch. If I had been standing, I would have punched him, whether it was hot or not. Instead, I let out a string of curses that would have made most women blush. Because really—*what the hell?*

The soft chuckle pissed me off even more. He set me back on my feet, crowding me against the wall before I could react. The warmth of his body added a confusing layer to our situation, as did his close proximity as he shushed me with his lips near my ear. The nip at my neck stilled my verbal barrage. *Did he just bite me?* My breath hitched as he slapped a strip of tape over my mouth, then bent and secured my ankles. My eyes went wide then narrowed as I telegraphed how much he would pay for what he was doing later.

"Lil." He chuckled again, seemingly finding the situation hilarious. Then he sobered. "You need to be quiet. I'm trying to help you." He lifted me over his shoulder, his arm locked around my legs like a steel band.

The stocking cap kept my hair from obscuring my face, and I twisted my head so I could see where he took me next. He'd tricked me. I would find a way to make him pay, not only for what he had just done but because something wasn't adding up with his stealth entry in the early hours of the morning when the house was asleep. *We are no longer friends.*

Wait, is he here to kill Benito? I wasn't opposed to that. It would have solved a huge problem for me.

The only reason I didn't make noise when he opened the hidden door to my room was because Benito would do something worse than Matt. I could feel it in my bones, deep in the portion of my soul that remained, the half that wasn't buried next to Mom.

At least one thing made me happy. Matt had closed the bookcase so that my secret entrance to the room wouldn't be discovered. My stomach ached from the hard press of his shoulder. My face was against his back, and his scent invaded my nose with each intake of breath, making my head swim from how amazing he smelled. *Ah, I'm not attracted to him. He's the enemy.* I needed to keep that in the forefront of my mind.

He moved swiftly through my room, down the hall, then the staircase. His goggles were on, but it was dark for me. I could make out shapes here and there, but with all the blinds and curtains closed, was no moonlight to help.

We backtracked to the rooms on the north side of the house, away from the foyer and dining room. Then we were in the study, and I couldn't figure out why until he lowered me to the floor, squeezing me against him as he opened the window. I wanted to laugh. *How the hell will he get me out bound like this without throwing me?* From the fall alone, there would be a trail, and if the guards didn't find us, then whatever imprint and damage I caused from the wipeout on the ground would point them to what had happened. He was screwed.

He stepped back, and I almost dropped to my knees without his body stabilizing mine. His hand shot out to steady me. My ankles were duct taped, one across the other, making it difficult to keep my balance. Before I knew what was happening, he spun me so my back was to him then lifted me and threaded my feet through the open window. I cringed at what was to come until I felt someone else's hands grabbing my legs.

For the first time, real panic coursed through me, and I stiffened. I hadn't taken Matt seriously, planning to make a break for it after we were near the edge of the grounds or when Benito's soldiers cut me free—the most likely scenario. But everything changed in an instant. *Who is Matt, and who is he working with?*

The farther out I went, the more my chance at freedom slipped away. As my shoulders passed the window ledge, Matt yanked my stocking cap forward so that it sat askew on my head, covering my eyes. Fear licked along my spine.

I'd seriously misjudged him. All the teasing and the times he'd talked to me, showing me I could trust him, were a lie. I was a fool.

I couldn't afford to wait to react. I yelled as loud as I could, but the sound came out muffled through the duct tape. A hand wrapped tightly around my mouth, silencing my voice even more.

"Thirty seconds," an unfamiliar man's voiced whispered close to my ear.

Until what? The next rotation of the guards? That has to be it. I struggled against my captor's hold then was passed to Matt, and his familiar intoxicating—*hated*—scent surrounded me.

His hands settled around my waist, and I knew what would happen next. Before he lifted, me I tilted my head back then whipped it forward as hard as I could. My forehead slammed into something solid. Stars burst behind my eyes, and my forehead throbbed.

What did I hit? His collarbone? I know he had to bend down to lift me, but I must have miscalculated my timing. And not even a sound of pain from him? I was pissed.

Good. Anger replaced fear. I could work with that.

Not breaking pace, he tossed me over his shoulder, and we were off and running. I gagged from the motion and the pain from his shoulder pressing into my gut. I was glad I hadn't eaten anything in a while. It would have come right back up.

While he ran, I rubbed the side of my face against his shirt in an attempt to peel the tape off. I just needed a corner or even a tiny bit of the edge to adhere to the fabric instead of my skin.

It didn't work. All I managed was to slam my face repeatedly against his firm back.

He ran for what felt like hours. The discomfort from how he held me warred with the familiar hand that splayed across the back of my thigh, his thumb too high along the inseam of my leg for comfort. It was probably a good thing I felt so horrid and worried about who he was and what his plans were. If I hadn't felt so terrible, I feared I would've squirmed just a little so the friction of his thumb went a little higher.

We stopped, and I groaned against his back. When he lowered me to my feet, my knees buckled, and I gagged against the tape.

"Deep breaths through your nose, Lil."

If he could only see my face, I was cursing him to hell with my eyes. His arm went around my waist, fingers curled against my hip as he held me against him. A tug at my hands, and the plastic snapped off. I was free.

Not wasting a second, I brought my numb hands around and aimed a fist at where I thought his head was. It was no use. He grabbed my wrist and restrained it. With the other hand, I dug my nails into whatever I could reach.

Like before, he managed to grab both my wrists and secured

them with a new plastic tie but this time in front of my body. I wanted to laugh at the mistake. I could get out of those. Not only that, but there was a knife strategically hidden on the side of my pants that I could access.

I would get out of it one way or another.

A car door opened, then Matt moved me again. I was lifted and placed on what felt like leather seats. The seat belt went around and then I heard the click of the lock. He shut the door then got into the driver's side. I couldn't sense anyone else in the car, and no other doors had opened. I did hear another car start a little way up the road. Maybe he only had one person helping him.

"I'm not going to take the tape off until we get to my place. Hang in there."

I yelled "fucker," but it came out as "huhher" from behind the stupid tape. He chuckled, and my rage cranked up a notch.

Twenty minutes later, he cradled me against his chest while we went through what seemed like an underground garage. Much better than being over his shoulder. Not long after, we were in an elevator. The doors closed, and with a whoosh, we went up. I tried to count the floors, but it was impossible. If I had to guess, I'd have said we were going to the top floor or close to it in whatever building we were in.

Once off the elevator, he walked another couple of feet then set me on a chair. Mistake. As he pulled the tape off and I swallowed the pain of a layer of skin being removed, my fingers curled around the small knife hidden on the seam of my pants. The narrow handle fit perfectly between two fingers, and I could punch and stab at the same time.

I lunged forward, the blade positioned to stab whatever I came into contact with. I struck something. He cursed. Elated, I went for another jab. He hit my wrist, deflecting the attempt. A sharp pain radiated from my wrist up to my arm, and I fell hard against the side of the chair. The motion shifted the hat and uncovered one of my eyes. Like a pirate, I stared him down. All the hatred I felt at the situation I was in burned like fire through my gaze.

He stripped the knife from my grasp. Blood welled through a slice in his jeans. I'd stabbed his leg. He grunted then whipped the hat from my head. "You know you leave me no choice now?"

Oh shit. I didn't like the look on his face. Frustration and exhaustion was evident in the shadows under his eyes. Maybe I'd pushed him too far. There was no doubt he could fight. He moved with the speed and agility of a trained athlete.

He crowded me and unsnapped my jeans. I jerked back as far as I could. It wasn't much as I was still seated. I pushed at his chest, a cauldron of anxiety building in me. "What are you doing?"

"Taking these." He pulled off my gym shoes, tossed them to the side, then cut the tape. I reacted by bending my knees and kicking out as hard as I could. He shifted faster than I could track then took advantage of my straight legs by yanking at the waistband. Another second, and he had them off.

"You won't get away with this." *Goddammit.* My voice shook with fear over what I thought he was going to do. His hands dropped to the tops of my bare thighs. As his thumbs rubbed back and forth, I trembled beneath his gentle caress.

"I'm not going to do anything to you." He reached over and grabbed a tan throw from one of the other armchairs. After he shook the blanket out, he laid it over me. "We have a few things to discuss before I take the zip ties off you."

"What are you planning?" I couldn't stop the note of panic that remained in my voice since he'd pulled off my pants. "It's doubtful Benito will pay a ransom."

"I don't want his money."

"Then what do you want?"

"You'll learn some of that in time, Princess. For now"—he drew me to my feet, and I clutched at the blanket with my fingers so it wouldn't fall—"all you need to know is that in three days' time, we'll be married."

CHAPTER TWELVE

LILIANA

Again, he lifted me, carried me through the open-plan living room, down a hall, and into a bedroom. He tossed me onto the bed then went to the door. I shimmied until I sat up, so angry that steam could have come from my ears.

He was certifiable. *How did I ever like him?* My traitorous gaze slipped to travel from his seriously gorgeous face—I loved that he'd shaved. *No!* He was dead to me. I needed to stay mad. Narrowing my eyes, I tried to tuck my legs under me then gave up as the blanket was wrapped tight. "Benito won't allow a hitman to marry me. You'll be dead before you open your mouth to say 'I do.'"

All he did was wink. The door shut behind him, and I heard the turn of a lock. My gaze dropped to the zip ties he hadn't removed. *What the hell am I going to do?* I'd exchanged one prison for another, and I feared this one might be the worse of the two.

Alone, I dropped my head to the pillow, the slow turn of the ceiling fan mocking me with each rotation. There was enough light from the one Matt had left on in the en suite bathroom to offer a mediocre amount of comfort in the strange room.

Tears gathered in my eyes, but I refused to let them fall. I hated feeling helpless. *What am I going to do?* My phone and weapons were in the pants he'd confiscated and my bag. Heat bloomed in my cheeks at the conflicting emotions I suffered. With his we'll-be-married crap, there was no doubt that he was my enemy, *so why am I still attracted to him?*

Enough time had passed since he'd left me here. I rolled off the bed, the soft throw tangling at my feet. Kicking it away, I tiptoed to the door and tried the knob. There was no give. He'd obviously planned for that, and my guess was he'd installed a bolt lock with keyed access on the other side. Too freaked out by the situation, I hadn't paid enough attention and missed a glance at the door's hardware when he carried me in there.

The plastic binding my hands was a problem I could rectify. It would hurt, but I had to get the zip tie off. Palms facing together, I used my teeth to pull the zip tie tight. Then I lifted my arms over my head. In a downward sweep, as hard and fast as I could, I brought my hands down, flaring my elbows out.

The plastic snapped. I was free.

Next, I went into the bathroom to inspect every drawer and cabinet, even inside of the toilet tank. Aside from a hand towel, there was nothing in there, not even a shower curtain. If there were knobs on the drawers, I could have unscrewed them. If I palmed the knob with the attached screw sticking out between my fingers, it would make an excellent weapon to hit him, stabbing and tearing wherever I struck. There weren't any, though. Not even a dresser in the room, and the end table lacked a drawer. There was a closet, though. When I opened it, my mouth hung open. Clothes hung from the hangers, and several pairs of shoes were along the floor. *Wait.* I peered closer, noting the frayed thread on the collar of a blue blouse. *These are my clothes!*

How long has he planned this?

Regardless, none of it would work in his favor once Benito caught up with him and made him pay. Antonio Caruso too.

They were both vicious, dead inside, and killed without mercy. I'd seen enough to judge their characters accurately.

I ticked through my other options. There weren't any. I knew without looking that we were high up. It would do no good to try to escape through the window. That would be sudden death and not what I was aiming for. Fine. It didn't appear that he would hurt me. And since he wanted to keep me as a hostage for whatever reason, I would make his life fucking miserable.

Decision made, I crawled back onto the bed and under the covers. I was exhausted, but with all the adrenaline, I wasn't sure if I could sleep. But I would need my mind sharp. I had to try.

It took five minutes for my body to relax and another few for my eyelids to grow heavy. My breathing evened out, and not long after, I sunk into oblivion.

The dream I'd thought would come after the dinner with the Carusos hadn't. Instead, it found me while I slept under Matt's roof and transported me through sleep to the worst night of my life.

Loud pops dragged me from sleep, and I sat up, shivering in the cool air in my bedroom. The nightlight glowed faintly in the corner. I jerked my gaze to the door. It was closed. I clutched my stuffed bunny to my chest, burying my chin between its soft floppy ears.

Should I get up and find my mom?

Men shouted. More pops echoed through the house in a rat-tat-tat. *Guns?* I'd heard them before. The noise sounded like it was coming from downstairs. *Maybe I should go now?* I sank my teeth into my bottom lip until I tasted blood. My legs wouldn't do what I wanted them to. I couldn't make myself get out of bed where it was safe and warm.

Please make it stop. Rocking back and forth, I sang one of Mom's favorite songs her dad sang to her when she was scared.

My dad didn't sing to me. And his friends were scary. I wasn't supposed to be around them. He didn't like it when I ran through the house, telling me that children should be seen but not heard. I don't think he even liked to see me, though.

I had a playroom on the third floor that he wanted me to stay in if I wasn't with Mom. I tried, but it got boring a lot.

My door burst open, and I jumped. Chills ran up my arms and legs, stealing my voice.

"Lily." Mom rushed inside, and I sagged against the headboard. Everything would be okay. "Hurry. I want to show you that secret room. The one you are never to talk about, remember?"

At my nod, she smiled. But it wasn't the way she usually did, with her eyes lighting up and crinkling at the corners. "Come with me, Lily."

She looked like how I felt—terrified. I put my hand in hers as she dragged me from the room. I couldn't keep up and tripped. Her hand tightened, and she took a moment to help me up.

Finger to her lips, she hushed me from making any noise. It wasn't unusual. I knew to be quiet. The only time I didn't have to be was when Sofia, Emiliana, Enzo, and Trey came over to play. The house was different then. So was my dad. Those were some of my favorite times.

Mom jerked my arm, crowding me to the wall. Her hand squeezed mine, and I had to bite my lip not to cry out. Then I saw what upset her. A man with a gun was coming up the stairs. Mom swooped me up into her arms. We rushed down the hall to her room. I knew where we were going. She'd told me the secret room was in her closet.

I looked over her shoulder. It was dark. Then I saw him. Not his face, though. Big. I trembled.

He pointed a gun at us. I whimpered, and Mom slammed into the door to her bedroom. It crashed against the wall, and she rounded the bed. We were in the closet. She set me on my feet.

Her back was to the open closet door. Then he was there, filling up space. There was no way out. I cried out. My body shook uncontrollably. Mom's gaze flew to mine, and she yanked me out of the man's sight.

Yanked from the dream into the present, I sat up, my fingers curling around the blanket in a death grip. Inky darkness met my eyes, and the terror of that night held me suspended. The scream pierced my ears. It was long and loud. Tortured. *Where is the noise coming from?*

Then I realized it was coming from me. I forced myself to stop. Convulsions shook me. Familiar aftereffects.

When the door crashed open, I jerked back, slamming into the headboard. It thudded against the wall. A man entered. Silhouetted by the hall light, a gun in his hand. It was too familiar. Too reminiscent of what I'd witnessed from my past. Throat raw from screaming, my flight-or-fight kicked in. I was on my feet, running at him before I knew what I was doing.

My fist flew at his face. He slapped my forearm away then wrapped his arms around me. I kicked back, my heel striking his shin. The low grunt sent a surge of satisfaction, however short-lived.

"What the hell is wrong with you?" Matt roared.

Recognition flared as he dropped me on the bed then reached over and turned on the side table light. I scowled at the lamp. I should have used that to hit him. But I hadn't been thinking. The dream still had me in its merciless grip.

"Let me go." Throat raw, my voice cracked. The tremors had set in, lovely fallout from acute fear.

Matt stood over me, his expression unreadable. He wore a pair of lounge pants and no shirt. Holy hell, he was cut. I jerked my gaze from his expansive chest and the display of chiseled abs then back to his face. His black hair was disheveled as if he'd run his fingers through it multiple times or had been in bed. My traitorous body softened, core heating. He had an instant panty-dropping effect on me, and until recently, I hadn't hated it. *I do now.*

I reached for the throw near the foot of the bed, needing both the warmth and a buffer from his heated gaze that crawled up my body in a slow perusal, starting at my bare legs.

The blanket was out of reach of my trembling, bloody fingers. I sucked in a breath, blinked, and my vision cleared. *No blood.*

I hated this. When I went that deep into the memory from when I was little, it was hard to ground myself in the present.

He seemed to come to a decision and grabbed the blanket then drew it over me. The bed dipped from his weight, and I gasped. *What is he doing?* Then he was next to me. Completely unnerved, I shifted to scoot away. His hand clamped on my waist and pulled me close. I was lying flush against him, chest to chest. Heat radiated from his body, urging me to curl against him.

My hands went to his chest, fingers splayed. *So warm.* I would push him away. Soon. The scents of rainforest, fresh, clean, and bold, clung to his skin, making my head spin. It was intoxicating, and I wanted to press my nose up against him and inhale long and deep.

"I've got you." Matt tucked my head under his chin, pulling me impossibly closer, while his hand rubbed soothing circles on my back. "You're safe."

Ironic. "Except from you," I whispered.

He didn't respond. Fighting the way he made me feel—safe, cherished—I tried to get information. Anything to help me get out of that mess. "Let me go. Benito won't allow us to marry. Renowned assassin or not, you don't have the kind of power he craves."

"What do you think he'll gain from our marriage?"

"Nothing. He wants me to marry Tony because that'll strengthen his empire by uniting our family with Antonio Caruso."

"And you want this?" His deep voice rumbled up his chest and sent a volley of shivers through me, causing him to tangle his legs with mine and share more of his warmth. He misunderstood, but I wasn't complaining, even though I should have been. I should have pushed him away rather than craving the closeness he offered.

"Not even a little," I growled. "Tony will never touch me." I planned to kill him as soon as he confessed.

"But you wanted to be alone with him the other night. What was that about?"

What harm would it cause if I told him? "We think he was the one to murder Marissa. I wanted a confession before I killed him."

"An eye for an eye." He understood.

"Of course." We were Mafia, after all. It was in our blood. If one wanted to survive that life, one embraced the dark side more often than not.

My sluggish brain swung to the other thing that had bothered me. "How did you get my clothes here?" I sensed the grin rather than saw it, my head resting on his chest.

"Remember that time you came out of the shower and found me leaning against the door?"

"Yeah."

"I'd thrown as many as I could in a bag and had tossed it out the window to the tree where Sal was. I'd planned to be in the hall and knocking on your door right before you came out of the bathroom."

"You don't sound very remorseful."

"You were in a towel."

I didn't have a comeback, too tired to maintain light banter. His hand continued to trace circles on my back, and I relaxed further. It'd been so long since I'd lain in a man's arms, and rarely for the entire night. Trust was hard to come by, and sleeping with someone left me vulnerable to attack.

What was odd was how protected I felt with Matt, despite my circumstances. My instincts kept telling me that he wouldn't hurt me, that whatever he was doing would work itself out. But I couldn't figure out how, and without proof from him that he would protect me from my father, from Antonio and Tony Caruso, I had no choice but to find a way to escape. My eyelids drifted shut. A couple more minutes, and I would untangle myself because the door had to be unlocked with him here. I would do it as soon as he fell asleep. The problem was that the heat radiating from him affected me more than I cared to admit.

CHAPTER THIRTEEN

MAX

I woke with sunlight streaming into the room and Liliana's soft body pressed against mine. Her pink lips were parted in sleep and so inviting that I wanted to dip my head down and brush mine across them. Silent, she looked like an angel with her stunning features and white-blond hair fanned over my arm and the pillow. But I knew if I kissed her, she would wake with the ferocity of a lioness ready for battle. Sexy as hell, but not the method I had in mind for that morning. Better to let her wake slowly and without help from me.

She was supposed to be a pawn. That was it. I wasn't supposed to fall so hard for her. It would have been a marriage in name only. And after, we could have parted ways. I hadn't thought I would have any interest in her beyond that. I was wrong.

The short time I'd posed as her guard gave me a minute glimpse into her life, a loveless and cold home where her father reminded her often that she was insignificant, worthless. Then there was the side of her with her friends, free and full of life. How she'd managed to grow into the confident and beautiful woman I held had nothing to do with Benito but her inner strength. She had heart, and I wanted to find a place within it. I missed the brilliant smiles she would give me. She didn't laugh or smile enough, but when she did, it was filled with such joy. I didn't understand why she was living under her father's roof if he made her life so unpleasant.

Benito poisoned all those around him. I had firsthand experience of that. Sal called after Lil was asleep, before she woke screaming, and relayed that there was movement in one of the warehouses. Another demonstration was in order. We were taking drastic measures, and by that evening, Benito would be short one more warehouse.

I checked her wrists, making sure she wasn't injured. I regretted taping her mouth and making her feel even an ounce of fear.

Lil stirred, snuggling closer, the side of her face pressed against my chest, and I closed my eyes, savoring the feel of her in my arms. At least in sleep, she was almost willing. A wave of longing swept through me. Things were going to change, more than she could ever imagine.

Liliana

*S*o warm. I burrowed into the heat, not wanting to wake up, but it was so bright. *It must be morning.* My fingers twitched, and I tried to lean back to stretch, but something held me in place. Confused, I blinked my eyes open only to see a male chest that I was using as a pillow. That didn't make sense. I was groggy. I needed coffee to function.

A few more seconds ticked by, then everything that had happened the night before flooded my mind, and I jerked my head back only to find Matt's gray eyes watching me. *No, no, no, no. This can't be happening.* Horror filled me. I couldn't even process why we were lying side by side in bed. *Am I wearing clothes?*

I glanced down as much as I could—I was plastered against him. Heat flamed my face. At least I had my shirt on. Our gazes clashed again, mine narrow and menacing. I'd planned on making our time together utter hell. I would deliver on that promise.

A grin curved his too-sexy mouth. *Why couldn't he be hideous?* It would have been so much easier to keep my distance from him. Instead, I wanted to trace his lower lip with my tongue then bite down on it until he reacted. I wanted to be kissed by him again. In his arms, I felt small but protected. I wasn't familiar with that feeling.

"Are you hungry?"

For you. Shit—I needed to get a grip. "Why? Is that how you plan to kill me? Poison? Seems a little passive-aggressive, don't you think?"

"We don't have to be enemies." His deep voice rumbled through his chest.

"Says the man who duct-taped my mouth, zip-tied my hands, and tossed me over his shoulder while forcibly removing me from my home."

His eyes crinkled at the corners. It seemed that I amused him, which wasn't my goal. I pressed my lips into a tight line and glared.

"You were hiding from your father. That wasn't home. It was a prison. Something you said as well."

"From one prison to another." I rolled my eyes hard and would have fallen from the swift dizziness it caused if I wasn't already lying down.

"It doesn't have to be that way." He got to his feet and offered me his hand. "Come on. I'll make you breakfast and coffee."

I almost leapt from the bed at the mention of coffee, my

kryptonite. With reluctance, I scooted to the edge of the bed, keeping the blanket over my legs. "I want my pants back."

"Those were... interesting." He chuckled.

Lovely. That meant he found all the weapons Sofia tucked away in them. They were our stealth pants—ready for anything. Maybe I'd get lucky, and he missed one of them. *Oh!* I had my watch on with the choke wire inside. I wasn't weaponless. There was my wit, too, which seemed to disarm him a little.

As he left the room, his back muscles shifted in an intoxicating way. My tongue almost fell out of my mouth. *Christ, he's just a guy. Why does he affect me so much?*

By the time he returned, I'd come to the conclusion that I would join him for coffee, if only to find out what he planned to do with me. I mean, marriage was out of the question. Benito would crucify him, and if not, I would. Plus, in order for the marriage to be valid in the eyes of the Mafia, we would need to have a Catholic priest marry us *in a church.* That wouldn't happen. He would be dead as soon as he set foot on the church's front steps.

He tossed the pants onto the bed next to me. I raised my eyebrows. *Does he think I'm going to put them on with him in the room?*

"The door out of here is locked. You won't find the key anywhere, and there is no other way out. I'll meet you in the kitchen."

In a ripple of muscle, he turned, and my mouth had ideas of its own as I croaked, "Put on a shirt."

His laughter trailed behind as he left the room, mocking me. If we were going to have an intelligent conversation, I needed him to cover all that up. I was going through a dry spell, and he was too hot.

Groaning, I tossed the blanket off and grabbed my pants. In the bathroom, I rinsed my mouth and finger-combed my hair. *This is ridiculous.* He needed to give me toiletries.

Once dressed, I left the room and went down a hallway until it opened up to a large living room and kitchen. Wall-to-wall windows took up one side of the room, and the view of Lake Michigan momentarily distracted me. The view gave me an idea of where we were. A fireplace was on the wall opposite the kitchen. White-and-gray veined marble countertops contrasted with dark-gray cabinets. A large island with wrought iron-backed stools separated me from Matt as he worked over a skillet on the cooktop—*thank God he put on a shirt*. The heavenly aroma of coffee lured me closer. *Gimme.*

I rounded the island, uncaring of anything other than finding a cup and creamer. A tall red mug was on the counter next to a matching Nespresso machine that was currently filling a second one.

He pointed at the red mug. "That's yours."

Not even sparing him or the eggs he was scrambling a glance, I wrapped my hands around the mug and took a tentative sip—caramel goodness. *Wait, what the heck?* I peeked at his. Black. No creamer added. None on the counter. But mine was made how I liked it. "You planned for me to be here. It wasn't a spur-of-the-moment thing when you found out I was missing."

He didn't bother to turn my way but continued to make the eggs. I waited. I had coffee to drink, anyway. He shut off the burner then dished the food onto two waiting plates, plopped a piece of toast and some fruit on mine, then put them on the island behind him. Then he looked at me. "Sit and eat. You can ask your questions after."

My stomach growled. I took another sip of life-giving brew and stared at him over the lip of the mug. *He better not say a word.* Lucky for him, he kept a straight face. When he sat down next to me and dug into his eggs, I set my drink down and did the same. *How long has it been since I ate? Yesterday morning, maybe?*

It didn't take long until we were both finished. He pushed

his plate away then stood. As he did, I curled my fingers around the fork. His hand covered mine before I could slide the utensil into my sleeve.

He winked. "I'll get that for you."

I wanted to kick him. There had to be a way out of there. He worked for Benito. The kidnapping wasn't known, so he would go back to work. My mood lightened. That's when I would leave. I could pick a lock. Easy. Done. I just had to wait him out.

I tracked him as he rounded the island, stifling a smirk. He was trying to be casual, nonthreatening, but he couldn't hide the predatory vibe or his sheer size. When he lowered himself onto the stool next to me, caging my legs in with his, my pulse kicked up a notch. It was weird, but I liked being close to him. No matter how deadly he appeared—and I'm sure was—he hadn't hurt me even when I stabbed him.

Wanting to appear at ease, I leaned against the counter. "You wanted to talk to me?"

"I do." He leaned forward, his elbow resting on the counter too. "You want to get away from Benito."

I pursed my lips. *Where is he going with this?* "Yes."

He nodded. "After being in the house with you and him for a few days, there were things I observed that didn't show outside of those walls."

I held still, refusing to give away any tells but wondering what he knew. My palms grew damp, and I fought against running my finger over the crescent-shaped scar near my temple. *Does he know about that night? About what happened after?*

"Benito doesn't allow you to have any control in that house, with the soldiers that are there to protect you. You're treated like a possession. Your value is in what you can bring to the table for him."

Widening my eyes, I cursed the influx of emotions that swam through me. I was tougher than that. I would not show pain. None of it mattered. Benito didn't matter.

"We don't have to be enemies. I can protect you from him."

I raised my eyebrows, shocked that he thought he would somehow go unharmed. "And who will protect you? Because when he comes for you, and he will, you'll wish you were dead." There would be nothing stopping Benito when that happened, and I would wish the same fate for myself.

"That won't happen. Give me two days. You're safe here. He has soldiers out looking for you, but he doesn't know where you are."

"And after that? What then? Will you let me go or keep me locked up here as long as you want?" I knew what he thought. By the third day, I would give in and marry him. There was no way in hell I would let that happen. At least if I honored the contract to bind me to Tony, I would be alone with him long enough to get a confession out of him. I did have the hairpin, after all. Then I would make him pay and reap the added benefit of being free from Benito. I'd still have the problem of a father-in-law, though, and Antonio Caruso wasn't a kind man.

What are two days here when out there I run the risk of being found and returned? "Fine. But I want something at the end of that time."

Dark promise flashed in his gray eyes, and my body heated in response.

"So long as it's within reason, I'll give you whatever you want."

"Not good enough." There was no way I would accept when there was that much wiggle room on his end. "You owe me."

"Then tell me what you want."

I ticked off my list on my fingers. "Freedom to see my friends, not to be locked up here, out of the marriage contract to Tony. Shall I continue?"

"I'll agree to you seeing your friends"—he held out his hand —"if you promise to stop fighting me, not to escape, and be honest while we get to know each other. Then they can come here on the third day."

"Of their own free will." I studied him, looking for any indication that he was lying. "And they can leave when they want."

"Yes. Do we have a deal?"

I placed my hand in his, ignoring the spark of electricity that traveled up my arm from the contact. "We have a deal."

I hoped I wasn't making a huge mistake.

CHAPTER FOURTEEN

MAX

I shouldn't have been sitting across from Liliana, indulging in her company. That wasn't the plan. Cristiano had volunteered to babysit her until the time was right. No matter how much I tried to distance myself, I couldn't. It had all started with that photo, which I'd stared at every night for a week and at breakfast too. Sal had said I was obsessed, and I'd honestly thought he used the term lightly.

The plan had changed. The guys stepped up, and I found the time to spend with her, to bring her to my side. If she agreed, I would give her the world. But I wasn't ready to tell her everything. She needed time to get to know me, and I wanted her defenses down. That innate sadness in her blue-violet eyes that called to me. The obvious reason was Benito, but I suspected there was more to the story. There always was.

"Aren't you expected at work?" The corners of her mouth twitched.

She thought she had me there. "Nope. I had two days off. Yesterday and today. We've got the entire day to spend together."

A puff of air pushed past her pink lips, drawing my attention. Her brows rose. "Planned for my capture?"

I couldn't have fought the grin if I tried. "Something like that. I'll tell you that things were intended to go differently than they are now."

"How so?"

"I wasn't supposed to be spending time with you, especially when there are... things that need to be done." That seemed to pique her interest. I had to give a little to get what I wanted. "Let's get some more coffee and sit out on the balcony."

We made another cup each and took them to the balcony facing the lake. The sound of waves crashing against the shoreline replaced the quiet inside the apartment. It provided a more relaxed environment, which I needed to get Lil's defenses to crumble further.

She took the cushioned chair with the ottoman and kicked her feet up, crossing them at her ankles. I waited until she took another sip before attempting to nudge her thought process where I wanted it. "Let's assume you got away with your friends' help and established yourself somewhere else. Potentially outside of Benito's reach."

"That was the plan."

I didn't miss the intended sarcasm but chose to ignore it. "He had a meeting with the cartel. Raphe Espinosa and his son. What do you think would happen if he called in a favor to them? If they found you, I guarantee that either your father or the Espinosas would locate you despite any fake ID you have or managed to obtain."

Her lips pinched. She didn't respond to my question. I was getting to her. Benito was like a caged animal, and there was no love lost between the two of them. What he would do was questionable. He might have brought her back, but what he would allow to happen to her along the way concerned me. I could tell by how her pupils shrunk that fear had a choke hold on her too.

Jose Espinosa had a reputation for breaking women, and he'd wanted her.

"I need you to think about this." I leaned forward, my elbows resting on my knees. "If Jose got ahold of you, and I firmly believe your father would condone this, you'd come back different. A broken, docile version would suit Benito better. He wants you to marry Tony, tying your family to the Carusos, but you're a flight risk and would fight him the entire time. He needs this. His business is in a precarious state."

"What are you talking about? What's happening?"

"There have been problems with some of his shipments and warehouses where they're stored."

She snorted. "I don't see how that would put him in a bad position. We have an endless supply of money."

She didn't know. "Your mom had an endless supply, as she was from the original Brambilla line. Your Sicilian grandfather cut Benito off after she died. But not you. There is a trust your father kept from you. He lied to you and refused to let your grandfather have any communication with you, or I suspect he would have removed you from the household."

I took her drink from her hands, as her fingers had leached of color from how tightly she'd been holding the cup. Setting it on the table, I took her hand in mine. "Are you all right?"

Her head reared back, eyes wide. "Am I all right? Um, no. I'm not. It's just another thing that Benito's robbed me of. He told me my grandfather didn't want anything to do with me, that he was the one who'd sent men to kill my mom and me."

"I know your grandfather. I can promise you that what Benito said is not true. Vincenzo loves you. He wanted to be a part of your life. Benito wouldn't allow it. He manipulated you to believe the worst of your grandfather."

A tremor ran through her hand. She pulled it away from mine, tucking it under her leg. "What is it that you're trying to tell me here? That I'm safer with you? I fail to see how you'll protect me from both Benito and the Espinosa cartel. What will you gain by keeping me here? And marriage is not an option. If we get married—and by some miracle, I say yes, which is highly unlikely—they'll kill you anyway. Then they'll have me. It won't matter if I'm a widow or not because you're not Mafia royalty. There is nothing that will keep them from coming after me."

"I made a promise to Vincenzo to protect you, and I plan to keep that vow. But there's more I need to tell you." She'd had enough dropped on her. I could give her time to process before I told her the rest. "Tomorrow. Give me that at least."

Shrugging, she leaned her head against the chair. "I want to talk to my friends. Seeing them the day you think we're getting married isn't enough."

"You can speak to them tomorrow. On the phone." That's all I was willing to give. By then, she would know my real name and what that meant to her. Before that happened, I wanted to remind her how she felt when I was just her guard, her ally. The attraction, the curiosity, and the kiss... I wanted that back. Not because of what she would learn tomorrow.

"Fine." She turned from the waves to face me. "Let's get to know each other. What's your favorite color? Food? Position?"

If she were trying to shock me, it wouldn't work. Our lives made sure we could handle anything that came our way. I was the same as her, Mafia born. "I'd have to say blue-violet."

She rolled her eyes. "Not going to work."

It would. "My aunt's sauce on anything, really. Pizza, pasta, whatever she made, I would eat. And position? Every single one so long as it's with you."

Heat infused her cheeks. "You don't even know me."

"I know enough."

A war of emotion played across her face. "Fine. I'll play along, even though I'm not positive about your endgame. I can't see it working in your favor unless my grandfather is pulling strings to help you."

I grinned. She had no idea. Part of me wanted to tell her who I was, how I'd grown up, but the other side insisted I wait. I wanted more time until things got crazy. I needed her to trust me again if I had a chance of having a life with her.

"My favorite color is blue. I don't wear it often, but it reminds me of lying in the grass and watching clouds cross the sky. It's peaceful, tranquil. Food? Lasagna. Easy. Positions"—she smirked—"you'll never know."

I would. Before she could fight me, I reached over and plucked her off the chair. Then I took her seat, rearranging her so that she was curled against me, her cheek on my chest and our legs entwined together. It was how we'd woken that morning, and I wanted more of it.

When she didn't protest, which was surprising, I ran my fingers through her hair, toying with the strands and indulging the fantasy I wanted her to buy into. I told her about my place in Italy. "Soon after we're married, I want to take you home. You can reunite with Vincenzo, spend some time with him." I hoped she would think he was the one helping me. In a way, he was. "I have aunts, uncles, and cousins that will want to meet you. You'll love them. They're all about family. My aunts will have a hard time letting you go. I own a villa in Mondello. If we can manage to extract ourselves from my family, we'll go there and enjoy the beach, the restaurants, and each other."

"You had me until the last part." Her voice was sleepy, relaxed, and she rested a hand on my chest.

Soon, she wouldn't push me away. "You once told me that you wanted a family. I would give you mine." They saved me, took me in, and made me who I was. "I owe them everything. I promise that you'll love them just as much as they will you. My Aunt Rosa will take one look at you, tell you you're too skinny, and make it her mission to feed you. You can try to leave the kitchen, but she'll have you making dough, then pizza, then sauce, all the while laughing and drinking wine. It's an experience."

"She sounds... lovely."

The wistful notes in her voice encouraged me. "Do you remember what it was like when your mom was alive?"

"Magical. She loved being outside. We would cloudwatch. When we spotted a shape that sparked our imaginations, we'd roll over then sketch it, adding in all kinds of details. We were at the beach as often as possible. Then there were trips to nature preserves, botanical gardens. We would spend all day there, picnicking, playing tag, drawing, and she'd teach me about the different types of flowers. She used to call me Lily."

"Was it just you and your mom?" I didn't think Benito would have accompanied them, but I wanted to know.

"And a dozen soldiers, at least. Benito adored my mom. He indulged her. But no, he didn't go with us, if that's what you're asking."

Not wanting to ruin what was happening between us, I shifted back to her grandfather. "Vincenzo has her paintings hung around his home and many stories about your mom growing up. I've heard a few. He misses her. And you."

Her fingers toyed with the hem on my shirt. "I'd like to see him." Then she tilted her head so that our gazes met and held. Longing reflected in hers. "Are you sure you can get us there?"

"What do your instincts tell you?" Growing up in that house with Benito, hers had to have been fine-tuned.

"You mentioned that holding me here personally wasn't in the original plan." She ignored my question. "What was?"

"You would remain here yourself. The building would be guarded, with no way out. After three days, we would still be married. The rest, I hadn't thought too much about until Benito was neutralized. I would have given you a divorce had you asked for it."

"And now?"

111

"I've spent time with you. Now, I want to give you everything. And I want the same from you. In time, if you find that you want a life with me, one with loyalty above all else, then I promise that you'll never want for anything, and I'll protect you against all enemies."

"I'm not sure what made you change your mind."

What indeed. I decided to offer her the truth. "From the first moment I saw your picture, I couldn't stop thinking about you. You haunted my dreams. The stories your grandfather told made you come alive in ways I can't explain. I grew up around people who were lucky enough to find the love of a lifetime. They would die for each other. I want the same with you."

CHAPTER FIFTEEN

LILIANA

A handprint of flour was on Matt's black T-shirt. I had some on my nose and wore a smile that made my cheeks ache. Music played over the sound system, drowning out the rain pelting the wall of glass windows in the living room.

We'd hung out for hours on his balcony, talking. I shouldn't have been so at ease with him. I mean, he was the enemy. He was holding me hostage. I couldn't leave. But then he'd brought up my instincts and how I should trust what they told me about him. Not once while he was supposed to watch over me did he make me feel in danger. With him around, I felt invincible.

I was buying what he was selling. While he stirred his aunt's sauce recipe and I chopped the mushrooms that I insisted had a place on the pizza despite his protests, I couldn't help but smile. We were having fun. I didn't worry and wasn't as defensive as I should have been. I mean, he freaking kidnapped me.

I wanted to believe him when he said he would keep me safe. It was either work with him or escape and try my luck, running and hiding. With the cartel as another obstacle, I decided to agree to his terms of looking at him as a friend and not an enemy for the next two days. It wasn't a horrible deal.

Setting aside the chopped mushrooms, I sprinkled flour on the counter to roll out the resting dough. The individual rounds were soft and beautiful. The yeast had risen perfectly. I dropped one in the center of the flour then grabbed the rolling pin.

From behind me, I heard laughter. "I thought you were Italian." His deep voice teased my ears.

I shot him an annoyed look over my shoulder. "I am. But I didn't have anyone to teach me how to do this."

He tapped the spoon, removing it from the sauce he was stirring. All amusement melted from his face. I turned away. Heat infused my cheeks. I shouldn't have said anything.

"Now, you do." He took the rolling pin from my hand then stood behind me. His arms came around me, and he placed his hands over mine. He pushed my fingers into the dough. "An inch from the edges is where you start." After each time we pressed into the dough, he moved our hands back and repeated the motion until we were an inch from the other edge. "Then flip it and repeat."

Once that was done, he positioned most of my fingers under the edge of the dough with two on top, while the other hand held the inside position near the opposite edge. "Now, we stretch the dough." We stretched it, flipped it up, then shifted to do the next section. Over and over, until the dough formed a round, flat shape with a thick edge to serve as crust.

To be honest, I wasn't paying attention to cooking with all that muscle at my back and his arms around me. My pulse kicked up a notch with each touch and every time his chest pressed against my back. As soon as we finished and he moved back, I shifted to the side. "Weren't you going to open some wine?" I needed something. Matt's body against mine, that rainforest-and-ocean scent that clung to his skin, and his sexy voice packed a mega-punch through my resistance. I wanted him. There was no denying it. There was also no giving in to that.

"Sure." He crossed to where the red wines were kept and pulled one out.

I needed the breather. If he touched me one more time, I was going to combust into a pile of ash at his feet. The cork came out with a pop, and I jumped. I felt his attention without looking. Keeping my head down, I stretched the second dough as he'd taught me.

The kitchen was warm, and I washed my hands as soon as I finished then twisted my hair up into a messy bun. The built-in pizza oven threw off some serious heat. I glanced at the ingredients as he set a glass of wine in front of me. I immediately took a sip. We had the sausage cooked and in a bowl, along with spinach, mushrooms, sliced tomatoes, onions, and pepperoni.

His back flexed as he bent to take the peel, the shovellike pan, from a lower cabinet. His shirt was too tight. *Maybe I should suggest baggy clothes.* I swiped at my mouth while he wasn't looking to make sure there wasn't any drool. The man was seriously hot.

"Ready to build the pizza?" His grin made him look boyish, in a way. Almost familiar.

I tilted my head, trying to place why I thought that. "You have a dimple!"

He shook his head. "Sadly. My cousins teased me about it when we were growing up."

I leaned a hip against the counter as he spread sauce on our pizzas. "It sounds like you had a pretty amazing childhood."

"For most of it."

What does that mean? I opened my mouth, but he popped a piece of pepperoni in it. Guess he didn't want to elaborate. We could talk about that later. It wasn't like we lacked time. I shifted so I was beside him, then added the spinach, cheese, and fresh sliced tomatoes to mine.

After he built his meat lover's pizza, he slid both of ours into the oven then took plates from the cabinet. The food smelled so

good, my mouth watered, which I fixed by having more sips of wine. By the time he had the pizzas out, I had to refill my glass. His was untouched. I pursed my lips, studying him while he cut the pizzas then put slices on each of our plates. *Guess I'll be drinking most of this tonight.* I plucked the bottle off the counter. *Fine by me.*

His movements were casual, even practiced. It made sense, as he'd probably made pizzas more times than I could count with his family over the years. A pang struck my heart, but I pushed it away to refocus on him. Something bothered him. He seemed preoccupied.

"Can you grab the glasses?" He glanced up then grinned at the bottle already in my hand. He took the plates into the living room and set them on the coffee table in front of the dark-brown-leather couch. I followed with the wine glasses and bottle.

After depositing his wine next to his plate, I sat on the couch, curled my legs under me, and took a slice of pizza. He did the same, and we ate in silence for a few minutes. When I finished my first slice, I took several sips of wine.

"Thank you for teaching me how to do that." I meant it. If Mom had been alive, I would have had extensive knowledge of how to cook authentic Italian dishes. My lack of cooking skills bothered me and made me feel like an imposter. "The sauce makes everything come together."

"Aunt Rosa would be overjoyed." He polished off two more slices, washing them down with a hearty sip of his wine before setting it on the table and facing me. "I was going to wait to tell you this, but I don't see the point anymore."

"Okay." I put my glass down and gave him my full attention. We'd had a great day, aside from the fact that I was there against my will. That was changing, though, if I was honest. Somehow, I believed he would do everything in his power to keep me safe. The bigger threat was Benito.

"Tell me where your head's at." He angled toward me. One muscular arm stretched out along the back of the couch.

"With what?"

"The wedding."

I snorted. I couldn't help it. "I find it very hard to see that happening. Benito is set on me marrying Tony. He'll eradicate any obstacle now that he's got the marriage contract in hand." I locked my gaze with his, imploring him to see that I meant every word. He needed to take Benito seriously as a major threat, regardless of my grandfather's help.

My thoughts strayed to the papers in my bag I'd taken from the safe Benito had stashed in Mom's secret room, but a wash of fear doused me. I couldn't do it. I couldn't see things ending well for me.

"Forget about Benito for a minute. Are you telling me that you can't love a lowly hitman?" His brow rose over those mesmerizing, sometimes-obsidian gray eyes.

I choked back laughter. He was serious. "I can love anyone, Mafia or not. That's not the issue. Who I will end up with is out of my hands."

"That's true, to an extent. What do you think of Tony?"

Rage, fast and furious, tore through me. He was a bully and horrible to his mom. What I wouldn't have given to have mine back, and he took his for granted. "I hate him. I would rather die than let him touch me. I already told you that I'm positive he killed my friend Marissa." I leaned forward, making my point clear. "And when I get him to confess, I will kill him."

He studied me for a second before offering a brisk nod. With his expression shuttered, unreadable, I couldn't tell if his opinion differed. "Forget about Tony for a moment. We'll come back to him and how to make him pay *if* he murdered your friend."

I clenched my teeth because letting go of my anger wasn't easy. I needed a distraction. My gaze crawled over him. The tight black T-shirt only accented his muscular body, and his jeans molded to his thighs. *Could I fall for him? Easily.* But I wouldn't let myself because if Benito got ahold of me, I would suffer for it and ultimately marry Tony.

"You're not marrying him."

"That's the plan. Doesn't mean I'll get my way, though."

He waited another minute, studying me before coming to some conclusion. "Did Benito show you the contract?"

I couldn't stomach the betrayal at the mention of the contract, Benito signing my life away as if I was nothing to him, and the fact was that I wasn't. According to him, I would never be as beautiful as my mother. I was worthless, not a boy, and also the reason my mother was dead. I needed another drink. I grabbed my wine and took a hearty gulp, hoping it would push the hated thoughts back into the box in my mind where I tried to keep them locked away and not rattling around in my head, mocking me.

"Tony's name isn't anywhere on the contract."

What? "How do you know that?" I sat up straighter, mentally reviewing what I'd read the day he'd shown me my future in the form of an arranged-marriage document. Benito would have secured that document so no one could get to it. The pieces clicked together, and I remembered. Tony's name hadn't been on the document.

"I have a copy myself." Something flared in his eyes. *Triumph?* "It specifically states Antonio Caruso's eldest son."

"And that's Tony." *What am I missing?* I held very still. The moment seemed poignant. I had to connect the dots, but for the life of me, I didn't know what he was talking about. I'd never heard that Antonio had another son. At least not one that was alive. But that's exactly what he was insinuating.

"You aren't promised to Tony but to Antonio's oldest son, Maximus Caruso."

"But he's dead. That would make Tony the oldest."

A menacing smile curved Matt's lips, and I sucked in a breath. *What is going on?* Lightning flashed, lighting up the dark sky in an ominous display, making Matt seem larger than life, deadly, someone not to cross. I wrapped my arms around my stomach.

In that instant, I had the sense that my life would never be the same, and a part of me was excited for the possibility of what that meant.

"He's very much alive. I'm Max Caruso. The contract is about us. There will be no contesting it when Benito learns who I am. And he will. If not before, then when we're married the day after tomorrow."

CHAPTER SIXTEEN

LILIANA

The shrill sound of a phone shattered the quiet room. Matt —no, *Max*—silenced it. I finished my glass of wine. Thunder rumbled in the distance, getting louder as the storm moved closer. The rain slammed against the windows in sheets as if desperate to get inside while I contemplated escape.

His news complicated things. What I wasn't sure about was whether it was for the better or worse. Arranged marriages were commonplace in the Cosa Nostra Mafia. Women were pawns, political ties between the different branches. I'd grown up knowing who I married wouldn't be my choice but merely to strengthen the Brambilla empire.

All my interactions with Matt—Max—replayed in my mind in a barrage of images. The way he angled his body around mine when we moved through people or the made-men in Benito's employ. How I felt secure with him at my back and side. Even when I'd attacked him, stabbed him, he'd never hurt me. Not really. The duct tape and running with me over his shoulder wasn't pleasant but also not meant to cause me real harm.

Aside from the obvious, I didn't understand why Max had

such a deep-seated hatred for Benito. It had grown evident over the past few days that it went beyond what he'd witnessed while working for him under the guise of a renowned assassin contracted by the Sicilians. I would have to find out why. Also, Max should have grown up under Antonio's care. It didn't make sense.

Max sat next to me on the couch, waiting, watching, while he gave me time to process this new information. I'd listened to what he wanted. At first, our interaction was to be more of a business deal—he would get what he wanted and I would gain freedom—but he'd changed his mind after spending time with me. He wanted a life together, a family. I didn't dare hope. Not yet. I could put concessions in place so that I was comfortable with our... partnership.

I opened my mouth to propose my list of demands when his phone vibrated. He glanced at the screen then answered as someone pounded at the door. Max leapt up, the phone pressed to his ear as he closed the distance to the front door in long strides. I twisted on the couch so I could see who was at the door—no reason to get up. I didn't plan on escaping. We had a deal to make. The more I thought about it, the more I liked my odds.

It took a few seconds for Max to get the key from his pocket —a safety measure installed with kidnapping me in mind—and unlock the door. He jerked it open, and a soaking wet man I'd never seen before stepped inside. He and Max exchanged hushed words too quiet for me to hear. The urgency of them, however, wasn't missed.

Something was very wrong.

While they spoke, I studied the unfamiliar man. The way he stood told me he knew how to handle himself. It was impossible to tell with his wet hair, but I guessed the color to be a dark brown, not black as it appeared. The sides were cut short, the top longer and mussed as if he'd pushed it back out of frustration. He wore a shirt similar to Max's and black pants. He held a 9mm and moved as if it was a natural extension to his body.

When Max glanced over his shoulder at me, I sat up straighter. "What is it?" *Has Benito found me?* The angles of his face were more prominent. Deadly retribution telegraphed from his taut features.

Whatever had happened, it wasn't good.

"I need to go out for a little while. You'll be safe here." Max left the guy at the door long enough to grab his gun before he addressed me again. "This is my cousin Sal. He'll stay here while I'm gone. You can trust him."

Sal grinned at me, and a brief flash of amusement swam through his dark, pain-filled gaze. "But can I trust you?"

Max said something else to Sal that I couldn't hear then was out the door. Sal locked it behind him then crossed to Max's room. When he came back, he had a phone in his hand. *Is that my burner?* I shifted to the edge of the couch cushion.

"Max said you could call your friends Sofia and Emiliana." I extended my hand, palm up, but he held it out of my reach. "But if you tell them where you are or give away any information other than your well-being, I will be forced to take it from you before you can get more than one incriminating word out. This is also for your safety. Do we have an understanding?"

"Yeah. Got it. Don't tell them who I'm with or where I am." I wanted my phone. They had to have been going crazy with worry when I didn't call them again. And it wasn't as if they could go to my house to see what the problem was. I pressed the contact button for Sofia.

"What's going on?" Sofia yelled upon answering.

"I'm okay. Hold on. Conferencing Em."

"What the actual fuck?" Em growled.

"Yeah, I know. I'm sorry." I closed my eyes at the fear I heard in their voices. They talked at the same time, making it impossible to decipher their words. "I can't tell you where I am. At least not today. I think. Saturday?" I looked to Sal for confirmation. He gave a brief nod.

"What's significant about Saturday?" Em snapped.

"And that's the day after tomorrow. Two days, Lil." Sofia added.

"I know. But I swear I'm safe." I grinned as my gaze landed on the pizza. "I'm eating homemade pizza and drinking a bottle of wine."

"Good wine?" Sof asked.

"The best. I've finished half already. Feeling great. I promise."

"We were in the process of rounding up the guys." Em's voice calmed, her tone serious. "Stefano was livid. He told me to stay out of it, that everything would be fine. What does that even mean?"

"I-I don't know." I'd assumed Em's brother wasn't on Benito's side. He was Frank Rossi's son, and my dad hated him. "Did he say anything else? I mean, had he talked to Tony, Benito, or even Antonio?"

"No idea. He was tight-lipped after that. But he did tell me that I'd better stay far away from your house for the next few days. He even put two of his guys on me. I can't go anywhere without them reporting to him."

"Sof, did you say anything to your brothers or Enzo?"

"No. Em got ahold of me before I could. If Marco went into alpha protection mode like Enzo—or even worse, all three of my brothers—then neither of us would be going anywhere. We figured we'd better wait to hear from you. If we didn't soon, we would have gone to the house, with or without the guys."

I loved my friends. I couldn't help but smile at the thought of Sofia and Emiliana breaking into my house and threatening Benito at gunpoint. "That would have been epic."

"Right? He has it coming, anyway," Sofia said.

Sal made a motion with his hand.

"I've got to go. Love you guys. Promise I'm safe."

After we all said goodbye, Sal took the phone back to Max's room. A few minutes passed before he returned, wearing a pair of Max's sweats and a dry shirt. When he went into the kitchen, he grabbed the last two pieces of Max's loaded pizza. He sat opposite me back in the living room on one of the chairs across from the coffee table. I pulled my feet back onto the couch and got comfortable, a fresh glass of wine in hand.

"You're from Italy?" His accent was more pronounced than Max's was.

Sal took a huge bite, chewed, then washed it down with a gulp of water. "Yeah. Max and I grew up together."

"Where did he go?"

Silence met my question. I tried another angle. "Will he be back tonight?"

Nothing. He finished off his slice of pizza then started on the other.

"Why are you helping him?"

That got his attention. "I would lay down my life for Max. So would the others. He's proven himself over and over to the family when he didn't have to. If you go against him in any way, know that it won't only be me coming for you."

Interesting. I opened my mouth to ask him another question, but he cut me off.

"And that's all I'm telling you. I'm here to make sure nothing happens to you while he's gone and that you don't leave."

"Noted." It didn't matter if he talked or not. I would get more information when Max came back. And we had things to discuss if I was going to be an agreeable participant in a marriage.

Sal picked up the remote and turned the TV on, flipping channels until he landed on an action movie. Not long after, a text came in. He swore, typed furiously, then waited for a response. When one came, he looked at it then shoved the phone back in his pocket.

"What's wrong?" A sense of urgency settled in as I thought about why Max had gone out. *Is Benito nearby?* "Maybe I can help?"

"Doubtful." He cast a glance my way, and the lines around his mouth eased. "But the sentiment is appreciated."

I didn't worry about the brush-off. Max and his cousin weren't Benito or even cut from the same cloth. In time, they would realize I was resourceful and a valuable asset.

CHAPTER SEVENTEEN

MAX

The speedometer read eighty miles per hour as I merged onto the highway to head to the affluent Chicago suburb where most of the Italian Mafia lived. Benito would know I was coming and have reinforcements called in. If that call had been to Antonio, it would save me an overdue chat with my father.

The wind pushed against the driver's side of the car. The few trees we passed bent with its increasing force. But as I sped along the highway, the storm lessened to a drizzle, and thunder rumbled in the distance.

About twenty minutes later, off the highway and deep in a wealthy subdivision, I stopped on the side of the road, out of visibility from the gated entrance to Benito's home. Seconds ticked by as my eyes strained to find my cousin. I didn't have to wait long before Cristiano separated from the shadows a ways from the gate then got into the passenger seat.

"He's holed up inside. More soldiers are patrolling the grounds, eliminating the gaps." Cristiano went into detail about numbers and positions.

There had been no additional contact from Benito and none from Antonio.

"Are you ready to do this?" I needed him to watch my back when we entered the property. It would have been foolish for Benito to attack, as he wanted an alliance with Antonio and I was tied to him. It didn't mean Antonio would side with me, but the jury was out on what would happen. They were feeling their way before striking, as they were unsure of my relationship with the original Sicilian families.

Back on the road, I turned into the drive and paused at the gate. Vinnie manned the post. I rolled down my window. Recognition flared, and he slung the machine gun over his shoulder so it hung at his back then approached the car. "Boss isn't happy with you."

I grinned. "He's about to go into a rage then."

Vinnie laughed then waved to another of the soldiers, who promptly opened the gates. He moved out of the way, and I took off down the long driveway, screeching to a halt in front of the house.

Cristiano and I got out of the car and went to the door with determination. The other guards eyed us warily, knowledge that I was Antonio Caruso's eldest no doubt having reached their ears. I knew the two at the door, and they waved me in. They must've had orders to let me pass.

My secret was out. It was time to play ball. Not bothering to ring the bell, I walked in. The men who worked there tended to leave the door unlocked, as they were stationed inside and out. I wove through them without being stopped. Vinnie must have notified everyone, including Benito, that I was en route.

It didn't take long to locate Benito in his office, puffing on a cigar, phone to his ear. Five soldiers flanked either side of him, guns at the ready.

As Cristiano and I crossed the threshold, I let my mask drop that I'd worn in his presence. Gone was the loyal employee. I stood before him with the authority and confidence of a soon-to-be boss. I was in his world now. "We have two matters to discuss."

Benito chuckled, secure with his men's guns trained on us. But I saw the rage burning in his dark eyes. "The way I see it, our business is concluded."

"You signed a contract that promised to deliver Liliana to me. I am well within my right to wage war against you, with or without Antonio's aid. The wedding is scheduled for Saturday, and as it's Thursday night, that puts you in a bind. Where is Liliana?"

Benito remained unaffected. "And the second matter?"

Tommasso. "You have one of my men. I want him back, alive and unharmed."

His chair squeaked as he shifted forward to lean on his desk. "Now, we're at the heart of it. We found your man at my south-side warehouse. In his trunk was a flamethrower. What do you think he planned to use that for?"

"Your buildings had C-4 planted in them. A flamethrower isn't proof he had anything to do with your recent business losses." But it was Tommasso's favorite weapon. It was clear I wasn't going to get anything out of Benito. "The rules of the contract are binding. I will deliver hell at your doorstep if you do not produce Tommasso. If word doesn't reach me that Liliana will be at the church Saturday, also alive and unharmed, I will destroy every business you have that's still standing." Since she was in my possession, it was an advantage I would use to eliminate his drug empire without his knowledge. My feelings were in line with Liliana's grandfather's. The Sicilian Mafia did not deal in the drug business. It was beneath us. I was back, and I would enforce that same code.

"I will see you dead before you get within a city block of either of them!" His jowls shook with the ferocity of his words.

Good. I wanted him rattled. To drive home my point, I placed my palms flat on his desk and leaned forward, my gaze boring into his with the promise of what I would deliver. "Thanks to you, I know where they all are."

I sensed Cristiano backing out of the room. He would cover us from just outside the office, his gun never wavering from those inside. My point made, I shoved off Benito's desk, pivoted, and left the room. Once I cleared the door, Cristiano followed, ensuring they didn't shoot us in the back.

My gut churned with worry over Tommasso. We moved through the house quickly, out the door, then into the car. The engine purred to life, and we tore out of there—no sense risking Benito's ego. But I was the Caruso boss's son, and Benito couldn't touch me. Problem was, Antonio didn't want me, and Benito had firsthand knowledge of that.

"Antonio's next?" Cristiano asked.

"Yes." I hated to go there. Stepping foot into the place I'd spent my first handful of years was challenging. But it wasn't my home anymore. I didn't think it ever would be, especially without Mom's laugher filling it. After observing Nicole, Antonio's current wife, at Liliana's, I wasn't impressed. The same could have been said about my half-brother, Tony. I'd held a small amount of hope we could be friends, maybe someday build on that and call each other brothers, but it wasn't looking like that would happen.

The miles dissolved under the Mercedes' tires while my mind continued to process all that could never be. I wouldn't write off Tony. Things could change. But Antonio, Nicole, and Benito would be treated as the enemy, and eventually, they would fall.

By the time we arrived at Antonio's sprawling mansion, I'd managed to lock down all emotion. We were there to deliver a message to the old man, nothing more. Nicole met us at the door on unsteady legs, the staff clearly having alerted her to our presence. An overly strong scent of booze preceded her.

"Maximus," Nicole purred. "It's good to finally have you home where you belong. When I heard—"

"Where's Antonio?"

She pursed her collagen-filled lips before crooking her finger for us to follow her. We passed through the foyer and into a living room, where she went over to the couch Antonio was seated on and perched on her husband's armrest.

My father's second wife was an opportunist. I would give her that. I needed to make this quick, preferably before Tony stumbled in on us. "I take it he doesn't know?"

"About you?" Antonio huffed. "Why should he? You rising from the dead changes nothing."

I smirked. "That's where you're wrong, old man. Things are going to change. Liliana is mine, per the contract. Tony will step down from his duties as underboss over the next few weeks, and I will take his place."

"That's not—"

"It will happen. Go ahead and test me. I have the backing of the original families and a majority of the Italian Mafia too." That was my cue to Cristiano that we were leaving. I had no desire to be in that home a moment longer. "It will be awkward if Tony shows up for a wedding, expecting to be the groom." I shifted to include Nicole, whose mouth was hanging open. *How did she not expect this to happen?* "I'm sure you wouldn't want that embarrassment for your other son."

With that, we made our exit. The hairs on the back of my neck stood at attention the entire time. I had no doubt I'd just started a war with Antonio and Nicole. I was ready. I hoped they brought everything they had to the table—it was long overdue.

"You know they're not going to take this lying down," Cristiano murmured.

"I wouldn't expect them to."

The adrenaline from both visits kept me fueled for the better part of the night while we checked out every possible location where Benito could have Tommasso hidden. With a heavy heart, we returned to the lakefront brownstone I owned, where Sal and Cris were staying on the other floors. After parking and trudging through the secure garage to the elevator, I wondered if Liliana had made her decision.

Would she be with me or against me?

CHAPTER EIGHTEEN

LILIANA

The elevator doors opened with a swoosh and pulled me from a light sleep. Or maybe it was when Sal rounded the couch and stood in front of me, a human barrier against whoever entered. The sky had lightened, and the storm no longer raged outside. I sat up and peered around Sal's broad back.

Sal's stance relaxed somewhat as Max and another man, tall and lean with piercing eyes framed in long lashes every girl would have envied, stepped into the open floor plan. Their faces were drawn with exhaustion, and when they met Sal's gaze, both of them flinched. Sal took half a step forward.

"You didn't find him?" Agony wrapped his words.

"We'll get him back," Max promised, that fierce determination I admired reflected in his expression.

I leaned against the cushions so I could see Max and the new guy better. Tall and leaner than Max, he had wavy dark-brown hair that brushed along the collar of his shirt. Piercing dark eyes met mine, unsettling me with their intensity. A second passed before he said, "I'm Cristiano, Max's cousin."

"Liliana, but you probably know that already."

His lips twitched, but he got control of them before smiling, a wash of sadness trickling back into his gaze. If I had to have guessed, I would have said he was a sharpshooter.

Sal and Cristiano went into the kitchen to make coffee—all three of them had been up all night, but I needed some too. It was my drug of choice, after all.

While the other two men were by the island, Max came over and dropped onto the couch next to me. I couldn't help but tease him as it was clear he was upset. "Aren't you worried I'll attack you?"

He snorted. "You already did."

"Speaking of knives, I'll be wanting mine back."

"I'll get right on that." Max braced his elbows on his knees then dropped his head into his hands.

I placed my hand on his back. "What's wrong? Maybe I can help."

He pushed out a heavy breath. "Benito has Sal's brother, Tommasso. Cristiano and I weren't able to find where."

"I'm so sorry." If something happened to Sofia or Emiliana… I understood his worry. And I knew firsthand what Benito's cruelty looked like. "I might know where he is."

Max's head came up, my hand sliding from his back. He leveled his gaze on me as Sal and Cristiano joined us. "How do you know where he'd take someone?"

I locked my muscles tightly. There was no way I would show fear over what had happened. Besides, I'd handled it, even if the situation continued to haunt me—not only the possibility of what could have ensued but the additional layer of truth I'd learned about how little protection I had at home.

"Dumbass took me there once."

Max's mouth quirked into that grin that made my heart do somersaults. A little more, and that sexy dimple would reveal itself.

I hoped he wouldn't find anything amusing after telling him

what Benito's soldiers had tried to do. "Joey. Remember him? The day we first met. I held a gun on him? I call him Dumbass. It fits, don't you think?"

Sal snickered while Cristiano's lips twitched. Max's eyes hardened. "Where did he take you? Let me rephrase that. What did he do?"

As his features turned menacing, my confidence grew. "Joey and another soldier had a thing for me. I can't remember the other soldier. Weird, but I think it's like my mind blocks it. One day, after I'd smarted off to them repeatedly, they picked me up from school and took me to the cemetery."

Sal and Cristiano's expressions matched Max's. Obviously, none of them liked where I was headed. Newsflash: neither did I. The other soldier was dead, so nothing for me to do there. But I'd gotten Dumbass back for his part in that afternoon, and every time I looked at him from then on, I made a point of dropping my gaze to the thick, ridged scar bisecting his chin.

"What did they do to you?" Max punctuated each word, his anger palpable.

"It was the other guy's idea. They took me into the family mausoleum. Inside and to the back is where the crypt is for the first Italian-American Brambilla boss." Our deceased relatives rested entombed behind granite walls or cremation niches. "I learned that's where Benito takes his most hated enemies so he can torture and kill them with our dead as witness. Twisted."

"Liliana," Max growled.

I huffed out a breath, not wanting to tell them everything. "They were both there. Joey stood back while the other guy slammed my head down on the coffin, held me there, and was going to..." I let the sentence hang. No need to admit it.

Max's knuckles went white as he clenched his fist. I could see the anguish etched in the lines on his face. "Did you kill him for what he did?"

"No. Benito did."

Through gritted teeth, he asked, "And Joey?"

"I gave him that scar on his face." I looked down at my hands, not able to stand the pity on their faces any longer. "He didn't kill Joey because he never touched me, just watched. Didn't help. But I didn't tell Benito that. As far as he was concerned, Joey was in the car and came running when I screamed to pull the other guy from me."

"Why? Wouldn't Benito have killed Joey if you told him they were both there?"

I shrugged. "I figured it would be more beneficial if I could blackmail Joey for his part. If he got out of hand, I would show Benito the GPS records I'd downloaded from Joey's phone that I held over his head." I'd made Joey's life hell. It was a smart play.

"How did he get the cut on his chin?"

I laughed, the satisfaction of carving his chin still managed to give me a sense of justice. "I was still wearing my school uniform, and since it was a skirt, I was able to grab the knife I had strapped to my thigh. I stabbed the other soldier. Sadly, it wasn't a fatal wound."

Dark promise flashed in Max's eyes.

I couldn't have stopped the grin if I tried at the memory of Joey's distress. Besides, the conversation needed some levity. "As I turned around, I clipped his chin, twisting the blade as I sliced, then took off running. I left them there, howling in pain. The other one was on the ground, bleeding and holding his balls."

Sal and Cristiano stood frozen by the end of the couch, their expressions matching the one Max wore. After that, their presence faded from my awareness. There was only Max.

"How did Benito react when you arrived home? There had to have been blood."

He had to go there. The smile fell from my lips, and I told Max, never once looking away. "He was very nonchalant about it. When I told him, he shot the other guy. But that was it. Nothing for Joey when I said he wasn't involved in that way. All he did was remind Joey I wasn't for him. Benito was pissed that they took me to the cemetery, though, but not for any of the reasons he should have been."

Max dropped to his knees in front of me, his hands gently cupping either side of my face. "I promise you, he will pay for what he did. You're with me now. No one will ever hurt you again."

When he rested his forehead against mine, all the tension in my body fled, and I could breathe easier.

There was a peaceful stillness to the cemetery. The scent of earth, grass, and freshly cut flowers permeated the air. The four of us trudged along a wet path away from the SUV that Max had insisted on in case Tommasso was so injured he had to lie in the back.

The grounds were mostly dark. Some of the mausoleums, including ours, had soft lighting over the doors. There were bench seats both inside and out for grieving family members. The structure's architecture included the Brambilla name carved over the arched entryway that was surrounded by columns. Flowers were planted in abundance, softening the experience as much as one could hope.

Cristiano and Max whispered to one another, then Cris jogged ahead while we slowed our pace. It didn't take long.

We stopped in front of the door where Cris waited, a guard with his throat slit at his feet. There would be more inside, and I understood the need for the stealth kill. Everyone but me had their guns drawn. I was a little jealous and missed the weight of mine. Max pushed the door. It didn't budge. "It's a code." I moved around him and pressed the correct symbols embedded around the outer edge of the door. A soft click sounded, and I was able to apply minimal pressure for it to swing open with ease.

The coppery tang of blood and sweat was faint but present, telling us that someone had been harmed there. Max stepped in front of me. It made sense that Benito would leave someone there, as his secret was well guarded.

The front room was empty, but I knew that wasn't where he would have been. Benito would have wanted the original Italian-American boss to bear witness to his acts. In a way, I'd always thought it made him feel less of an imposter, a byproduct of being beneath my mom when he married her. It was another reason he'd set foot back in Italy only once.

"Stay here," Max whispered.

I didn't have any problem with that. I didn't want to be there. He motioned to Sal to remain behind, as well, probably so he and Cristiano could focus on taking out whoever was left behind to guard their cousin. We were looking for Sal's brother, and I understood the emotional hell he was in.

Sal backed me up toward the wall near the door, putting his body in front of me as gunshots echoed through the space. The sound of a fist hitting flesh ensued, then silence. With his body blocking me and his gun pointed at the entrance to the back room, we waited.

"Come back." Max called.

Sal and I hurried to him. When we arrived in the back room where the crypt was, I gasped at what I saw. Sal rushed to Tommasso with Max and Cristiano not far behind. I held back, horrified. Chains wound around him, holding him to the chair. His head was bowed forward, and blood saturated his shirt, dripping to the cement floor below and forming a small puddle around him. Sal gently lifted Tommasso's head, and no one spoke for a second. Both of his eyes were swollen shut. It looked like a heavyweight fighter had hit him repeatedly. Where the skin was taut over battered areas, it split.

Three dead guards were scattered around the room, one of them Joey. Blood marred his face—the reason I heard the punches. One less problem for me, as Joey would never bother me again, and further proof of Max's protection.

I scanned Cristiano and Max for injuries then dismissed them as they seemed fine. My gaze swung back to the beaten man not far from where I stood.

"Is he...?" I couldn't say it. Tears leaked from my eyes, and I didn't bother to wipe them away.

"No." Sal's voice broke.

They worked furiously to get him free. Cristiano found bolt cutters in the corner of the room where a suspicious cache of tools was piled. I didn't want to look too closely.

When he was unbound, Max and Sal carried him while Cristiano covered us. I wasn't okay with that and took Max's gun from where he'd stowed it in the waistband of his pants. No one said a word against it.

Our small brigade slowly made our way to the SUV, where they gently placed Tommasso in the back. Sal climbed in next to him, applying pressure to the worst of the wounds. Once we were all inside, Max made a U-turn toward the exit.

"We're going to have to take him to the ER," Sal said from the back.

"I'm headed there now." Max exited the cemetery and sped down a road that would take us to the highway.

"Are you kidding?" I shot Max an incredulous look, barely refraining from rolling my eyes despite the gravity of our situation. "We don't do that."

"You forgot that we don't have the connections here that we do in Italy," Cristiano added from behind me.

I grabbed Max's phone from his pocket. "We have a surgeon in the family." I dialed Trey's number and specified what we needed. "He'll meet us at your place, Max." I got the address to his place and relayed it to Trey. Once I hung up, I turned to each one of them in turn. "Now you have connections here too."

By the look on both Cristiano and Sal's faces, I knew I'd won them over. When Max took my hand, that was it for me. I decided then and there to make it work between us because I was already halfway in love with him.

CHAPTER NINETEEN

MAX

S team trailed me after my shower, and I left the bathroom, dressed in black slacks and a button-down. It was Saturday, the day of our wedding. The sun hadn't risen yet, and the main room was dark as I crossed to the kitchen to get a to-go mug brewing for Liliana.

I scrubbed a hand over my face, shocked at the turn of events the day before. After Lil had called Trey La Rosa, Sofia's brother and the Mafia's surgeon, my cousins viewed her in a new light. She'd welcomed Trey, rushing him to Tommasso's side and taking charge of everything. If Trey needed something, she got it. When Sal looked like he was about to fall over from worry and exhaustion, she'd made him something to eat and talked to him to ease his fear.

Sal, Cristiano, and I had gotten Tommasso cleaned up as best as we could and disposed of his torn and bloody clothes. He was in bed, wearing a pair of boxers only. Ugly bruises covered one side of his chest, and we worried about a collapsed lung.

She could have escaped while we tended to Tommasso. None of us would have stopped her, as our focus was solely on our cousin. But she hadn't.

Trey resembled Sofia with his dark hair, eyes, and easygoing manner until he got to work. Then he was all business. He set up an IV and started the drip with fluids, and antibiotics were given. Not long after, we had a diagnosis. The lung wasn't punctured, but he had three broken ribs and two busted fingers. The swelling on his face was extensive. Trey closed multiple lacerations then made sure I also had his number to call if Tommasso took a turn for the worse, but he thought he would recover in no time as long as he got plenty of rest.

We were indebted to Lil, but when Sal said something to that matter, she'd brushed him off. It was a turning point for all three of them. I was already committed to helping her, and after what she'd done for us, my cousins were as well.

I glanced at the time. I needed to wake Liliana.

I rapped my knuckles against her closed door. When she didn't respond, I let myself in. Light from the main room trickled in enough that I could see the outline of her body sprawled across the bed. Her hair was a wild mess over the pillow, and I loved it.

"Liliana, you need to get up."

She sprung up. Once sitting, her hand flailed around on the nightstand, probably for a gun. I flipped the light on, blinding us both. I would have crossed the room and gone to her, but in the state she'd woken, I would've caused her even more alarm.

After shoving her hair from her face and blinking slowly to adjust, she focused on me. "Max?" Her soft, raspy voice was sexy as hell from sleep. "Is Tommasso okay?"

I nodded. "He is." I moved to her bed, sitting so we faced each other. "We never got a chance to finish our discussion about the contract. I meant what I said. Once we're married, everything will be different. I won't keep you in a cage. You'll have freedom and protection. All I ask is that you're loyal to me."

I swore that time stopped. I'd thought she was beautiful

from the moment I'd seen her picture, and her haunted eyes called to mine. But when she smiled like that, there wasn't anything I wouldn't do for her.

"I'm all in. But no more locking me in or taking my gun."

"Your bag is next to the coffee, gun inside." I took her hand in mine. "There is a very good chance something will go wrong today, and I don't want to take any risks with our marriage license. We leave for the church in five minutes. The priest is waiting for us in secret. We'll be married this morning then again in front of everyone at noon." A very generous donation had been made to the church.

"Oh. Okay." She pulled her hand away and slid her legs over the bed until her feet hit the floor. "Give me a minute, and I'll meet you in the kitchen."

"There are some clothes in the closet."

We left a few things unsaid, and I'd woken her early enough to talk about some of them. I knew she needed to hear how I felt about her. In time, she wouldn't doubt what we had. I left her to get ready and returned to the kitchen.

We would leave after we talked. No matter how much I wanted to rush Liliana to the church, I owed her an explanation about where I had come from and why. When she came in, I handed her the coffee and guided her to the couch where we sat. She faced me, angled so that her back was against the armrest. There was space between us, and I hated it, but I couldn't do anything but tell my story.

I wanted to take her in my arms and make her forget everything but the two of us. A part of me knew it was better to have everything out in the open.

I took her hand, setting the tone with an inquiry. "What did you know about my mom and me before you and I met?"

"Not much. Maria was Antonio's first wife and your mom. You both died in a car accident. No one had heard differently until you returned."

That had been what Mom's family wanted, to keep my survival a secret, and I was glad to hear that there hadn't been any leaks. It had made my return what they'd hoped for me. I met her blue-violet eyes, ready to let her fully into my world. "I was six years old when my parents went to Sicily. Mom had a lot of family there, and she missed them. That was the purpose of our trip."

"The family you were raised by? Aunt Rosa and the cousins that came here with you?"

"Yes." I cleared my throat. That part still managed to send a volley of anger through me at the thought of what Antonio had done. "It was never proven that the accident was anything more than that."

"But you think otherwise?" She tucked her legs under her.

"I do. Benito and your mom were there. Our moms were childhood friends. From what my family told me, they spent the morning reminiscing about their past over coffee. When she was ready to go, my mom collected me from where I was playing in my room. I can't prove anything, but Benito was there when we got to the front door with keys to a red convertible. There was no driver. Antonio was in a meeting the entire day. He didn't even know my mom took me shopping."

She sat up straight, horror swimming through her wide eyes. "Do you think he did anything to the car?"

My hand curled into a fist. "I don't know. It was a hit-and-run. We were pushed off the side of the road and rolled."

"I'm so sorry, Max." She leaned forward, taking my other hand in hers.

I threaded our fingers together and pulled her closer. I remembered parts of the accident. Screaming then the silence when I came to. There was so much pain. Blood was everywhere. Mom's sightless eyes. "I came to only briefly in the car then not again until much later in the hospital with all these machines hooked up to me. My legs were broken. The first time

AMY MCKINLEY

I surfaced, no one knew about it. Antonio was there, and so was Benito."

"Oh, God. What did Benito do?"

"They were talking about my prognosis. Each day I remained in a coma was a concern. Benito told Antonio that he should leave me there, that it wouldn't be long before I died. I guess the doctors told Antonio my chances of recovery were low due to head trauma."

"Did he..."

"Yeah, Antonio agreed. He left me to die. As far as he was concerned, I was already dead the way I was. He needed a strong son, not one with a chance of brain damage if he ever recovered."

"There's nothing wrong with you. Didn't your family in Italy contact Antonio to let him know you'd survived and were fine?"

I shook my head, grateful for their past insight. "No. My mom's parents put a call in to family who had been out of the Mafia's sight for a little over eight years. I spent part of my recovery with them off-grid. When I was healthy enough to return to Italy, we did so as a family. They took me in as one of their sons. There, I was known as Matteo, and I became an assassin for the Mafia. Only mom's family and Vincenzo knew who I truly was."

"Wow. Aside from such a senseless tragedy, I have to wonder if your life was better there than it would have been if Antonio had brought you home."

I ran my thumb over the back of her hand, enjoying the softness of her skin. "I agree. His second wife is a train wreck, and Tony... so far, I'm not impressed."

"You shouldn't be. Tony's a very entitled and cruel man. It's rare for him to put anyone else's feelings over his. I honestly have a hard time seeing him taking over for Antonio." She pursed her lips, and a beat of silence fell between us. "I get that

144

Tony is your half-brother, that he's family, but I still have unresolved issues with him, as I'm sure you do with Benito."

I grinned. Emotionally tying my vendetta to hers was a nice play. I would have understood regardless. My cousins were more my brothers than Tony. "It'll all work out, so long as we have each other's backs."

"Always." Her voice was whisper soft.

My cell pinged, pulling us from the moment we'd shared, a text from Cristiano to tell me he was waiting in the garage. "It's time to go."

When we rose from the couch, Liliana wrapped me in her arms, hugging me with her whole body. No words were needed. After we drew apart, she made a beeline to refill her mug. Her hair was brushed and shimmered down her back. The only makeup she wore was mascara and a coat of soft pink lipstick. In a white sundress with little flowers, she was a vision. She slid her arms into a thin white sweater wrap then added her backpack over her shoulders. Coffee in hand, she stilled. "Ready?"

"Yes. Cristiano is in the garage. We'll come back here after, eat, and check in on Tommasso."

"Okay."

I settled my hand at the small of her back, unable to resist tugging her against my side. The memory of our first kiss, while she'd thought I was Matt, was seared into my mind. I looked forward to the moment the priest pronounced us as husband and wife and what would follow.

We rode the elevator down in silence while Lil took sips of coffee and seemed content to lean against me. We exchanged greetings with Cristiano, and then we were in the car and en route to the church as the sun rose on the horizon. It was a big cathedral with ornate Gothic-style architecture, where the Cosa Nostra held many wedding ceremonies. I pulled around to the rear lot, and we slipped in through a back entrance.

The hallway and rooms were dimly lit in preparation for our

arrival. When we entered the vestibule, Lil stopped short, a gasp leaving her lips. "When?" She turned to me, tears in her eyes. "I called a favor in to Stefano." I cupped her cheek, her skin like silk against mine. Her face was upturned, and I leaned down, brushing my lips across hers in a gentle caress. "I know this isn't the wedding you dreamed of, so I had to do something to make this special for you."

My chest tightened when she didn't pull away. I wanted to deepen the kiss, but we were on a time limit. I drew her down the aisle lined with hundreds of candles in various heights to the altar. Surrounding the priest, more candles blazed, bathing the room in a warm, ancient light that spoke of weddings of the past. The church was ancient, and it was easy to imagine how it would have looked hundreds of years before.

"Stefano." Liliana acknowledged the Rossi underboss. "Thank you for being here."

"My sister would have wanted me to. It's an honor, Lil."

A tear rolled down her cheek at the mention of Marissa. She went up on her toes and hugged Stefano. When she released him, she returned to my side, clasping my hand in her smaller one. We approached the priest, who had bushy snow-white eyebrows and a map of wrinkles that told of a long life. We stood before him with Stefano and Cristiano bearing witness.

In a truncated version, we said our vows and were pronounced husband and wife. I bent and captured her mouth. She parted her lips for me as her arms wrapped around my neck. Passion flared at the first touch. As I deepened the kiss, all I wanted was more of her.

"Congratulations, Max, Lil." Stefano clasped our hands.

"Glad to have you in the family." Cristiano hugged Lil then me.

The priest signed and handed over the marriage certificate that gave Liliana the protection of my name, the ink not even dry. He had another copy that would be filed. "We'll see you both back here in a couple of hours."

After thanking him for performing the dual ceremonies he had on the day's agenda, we took our leave. The car ride home was quiet. Lil didn't seem tense, but I wondered what was going through her head until she turned to face me. "I don't feel married."

I grinned. "Yet." If I had my way, she would feel married that night.

Liliana

The sun was up, and the scenery flew by as Max maneuvered the sleek car through the streets and then to the secure underground parking beneath his building. I waited for him to open my door and offer a hand as I got out. My fingers wove together with his as if it was the most natural thing to do. He pulled me into his side in the elevator, and my arm went around his waist instead of holding his hand. He bent to murmur near my ear, "Why don't you go on up to our floor? I want to check in on Tommasso and will follow soon."

Our floor. A thrill raced through me at his words. I agreed, and Max and Cristiano got off on Sal and Tommasso's floor. As the door shut, I was whisked up two more flights then got off. Once the doors closed and I was alone in the living room, I about squealed with excitement. In a way, I was freer than I'd ever been with Benito. Time would tell for sure, but I felt comfortable with Max. He'd told me he wanted a partner, not a prisoner. I believed him.

All I had to do was look at his actions, which told me everything. I threw my head back, and a carefree laugh tumbled from my mouth. I'd dodged a bullet by marrying Max rather than

Tony. I bet Benito was blowing a gasket. With Max, there was no way Benito would gain anything. Max would ensure that. It was clear he hated my father.

When the elevator pinged and the doors opened, I whirled around. Max strode toward me, and all thoughts fled my mind from the intensity of him. "How's Tommasso?"

"Sleeping," he managed to get out before his hands were on either side of my face. Then he bent to take my lips with his.

I melted against him, my hands clinging to his waist, and my heart and body took over. His tongue danced with mine, exploring. In our kiss, I tasted the promise of real love, years of passion, happiness.

By the time he broke the kiss, my knees were weak, and my mind a haze of desire. *Do we have to go back to the church?* I sank my teeth into my lower lip, my pulse a crazed beat at the base of my neck. *We could stay here and make better use of the time we have before whatever fallout occurs from Benito.*

That last thought was like a bucket of cold water. "When do we need to leave?"

"Not for a couple of hours. We have time to shower, eat, and relax." He tucked a strand of hair behind my ear then frowned. "What are you thinking?"

"I'm worried about what Benito will do. And I don't even know what the deal is with your situation with Antonio." I paused for a breath. "Also, how do you know Stefano well enough for him to be a witness at our secret wedding?"

"I know Stefano from when he came to Italy to find Emiliana when she was abducted. And if Benito tries something, which I don't think he will, it invokes part of the contract he signed that leaves him vulnerable. What could happen is retaliation from the Caruso family. But I'm not worried."

"I am—"

"I'll keep you safe."

"I know." And I did. Even if he could have handled things differently, that was something I carried no doubt over.

He slid his hands down until they were on my hips. "I want this day to be just about us."

He rested his forehead against mine, and in that moment, I would have promised him the world.

CHAPTER TWENTY

LILIANA

When we arrived at the church for the second time that day, Max parked in the front. Cristiano and Sal were a minute or two behind us. We'd spent the time before we were due cooking lunch together and talking. It had settled my nerves and only helped to bring us closer together. I'd also learned that Max and Stefano had men stationed around the church, which went a long way toward easing my mind.

I wore the same sundress because he said my wedding dress would be at the church already. When he'd asked if there was anything specific I wanted for our wedding, I'd told him it was important to me that Sofia and Emiliana were there.

As we climbed the stairs to the church's ornate door, the heat of his body blanketed mine, reminding me of what we'd looked like when I saw us in the mirror at my house and how protective his posture had been. A sense of belonging filled me. He was giving me more than my own family ever had. Already married, we didn't need to go through with the formality of an elaborate ceremony, but we were, and I knew he was doing that for me.

A car screeched to a halt, and we both whirled around. Max

dropped his hand from my waist. He pulled out his gun then sidestepped in front of me just as Tony leapt from the car.

A second car flew toward us, its tires squealing as it came to an abrupt stop. My gun was in my backpack. I couldn't get to it quickly enough. Doors opened, and Sal and Cristiano hurled themselves from the car, their guns raised, aimed at Tony.

"Back," Max said underneath his breath, and I reached behind him, taking his other gun from the waistband of his pants. From behind Tony, Cristiano and Sal closed the distance, their expressions deadly.

A grin stretched my mouth wide, and I laughed. It wouldn't have been a Mafia wedding without someone pulling a gun. I shook my thoughts away. There was a threat that needed to be dealt with.

The commotion behind Tony didn't faze him. He stood, arm outstretched, gun aimed at Max. Sal drilled his 9mm into the back of Tony's head. He froze but didn't turn. Rage painted his face a deep red. "You will not take what's mine."

"Liliana was never yours," Max countered. "You're outgunned. If you shoot me, they'll kill you."

I pressed my palm against his back, balancing on the balls of my feet. He was rigid. We were ready. If Tony wanted to go through with what he had planned, we would rain hell down on him.

A squeak sounded behind me, and I took my eyes off Tony for a brief second. The door opened, and Em and Sofia slipped through, guns in hand. "We saw through the window."

With the distraction of Em and Sofia, Cristiano wrenched Tony's arm back. A cry of frustration left his lips as he was disarmed. Cris pushed him away, and Max prowled forward with me on his heels until Em grabbed me. "Let him handle it."

"It's your wedding day. No need to get blood on your dress." Sofia winked.

Then Max was in front of Tony, threatening him for pulling a gun on us.

"You won't take my legacy. This is mine. All of it," Tony said with a growl.

"What's yours?" Max got in his space. "The Brambilla family? Or running ours?"

"You're not a Caruso and will never be boss." The sunlight reflected on the knife.

I couldn't help the gasp that escaped my lips. Tony's arm pushed forward, Max's neck the target. Max twisted, his forearm blocking Tony's strike. Sofia, Emiliana, and I strained forward. Then Max's arm reared back, and he slammed the butt of his gun into Tony's temple.

Tony crumpled to the ground, unconscious. Max turned on his heel while Cristiano dragged Tony away.

Amusement sparkled in Max's gray eyes, and I couldn't help but laugh as the tension fled my body. He closed the distance between us. Throwing my arms around him, I pressed my lips to his. When I pulled back, he grinned then took my hand.

"We have a wedding to go to. Let's do this." Under his breath, he whispered in my ear, "I want you all to myself after."

We all stowed our guns, and everyone piled inside the church.

The ceremony wouldn't start for forty-five minutes. Max accompanied me down the hall, showing me to the room where I would get ready. When he edged toward the door, I was engulfed in my best friends' arms.

"What?" Sofia pulled back. "You honestly thought we'd let you get married without us?"

Emiliana laughed then ushered Max out. When the door was closed, she waved me to the other side of the room. "We have a lot to do. Take a seat."

Sofia gave me a nudge, and I complied, sitting in front of a mirror framed in lights. The room was done in a pastel yellow with comfortable seating, a tiered mirror and raised platform, makeup station, and attached bathroom. Enough weddings were held there that the room had had a makeover years before.

"We have a makeup artist and hairstylist coming in five minutes, but we wanted to show you this before they got here." Sofia's excitement was infectious, and I shifted to the edge of my seat. She went into the bathroom and took something off the back of the door. "What do you think?"

"Oh." I was on my feet and in front of the gorgeous dress she held before I knew it. "You made this, didn't you?" At her nod I wrapped her in a hug, the dress between us.

"Lil!" She nudged me back. "You'll wrinkle it. Well? What do you think?"

"Please." I couldn't have wiped off the grin if I'd tried. "You know it's beautiful. How did you have the time? I don't understand." Intricate lace and beading decorated the spaghetti straps, plunging neck bodice, and tulle skirt of the ivory gown.

She rehung the dress then handed me a white silk bathrobe. I stripped out of my clothes and put the robe on, ready for all the primping that would follow.

"It was one I was working on for the fashion show in Milan. It's perfect for you. I'm glad I'd started on this one rather than one of the other sketches I was thinking about."

Emiliana opened a bottle of chilled white wine she got from the fridge. As she poured three glasses, a soft knock sounded. We all aimed our guns at the door. "Who is it?"

"Nico. Open the door."

Em let Sofia's brother in then put her gun away. "Food!" She grabbed the tray then set it on the coffee table in front of the couches. He'd brought sliced fruit, cheeses, crackers, and another bottle, which Em motioned for him to put in the wine fridge.

After Em gave us our wine, she poured one for Nico. When

he took it, she ran her fingers over the lapel of his suit. "Looking fine, Nic."

I stole a glance at Sofia, who'd bowed her head to hide the smile playing around her lips. Nico was putty in Emiliana's hands, but we'd always joked that he wouldn't know what to do with her. And he was safe, the reason Em was able to play around with him.

When she dropped her hand and sat on the couch, crossing her long legs, he tore his gaze away. Then he was in front of me, drawing me to my feet and wrapping me in his arms. "Lil. We're all here for you. Anything you need." When he pulled back and I looked into his beautiful brown eyes, so much like his sister's, mine got misty. "Any one of us, Dad included, would be honored to walk you down the aisle. Just say the word."

Oh God. I forgot about that. The thought of Benito walking me down the aisle almost made me sick to my stomach. He would be in close proximity to me and could do anything to stop the wedding. "Is Benito here?"

Nico nodded slowly, warily measuring my reaction.

"Okay, that's fine." I shouldn't have wanted his absence on my wedding day, but I did. My gaze whipped back to Nico's, and I took his hand in mine. The La Rosa family understood more than the others, as Sofia confided in them. It didn't bother me—they'd been there for me time and again. "Thank you. I can't even begin to tell you how much your family's offer means to me, but we both know what I need to do." It was best that way. Otherwise, the La Rosa family would be in Benito's crosshairs, and I couldn't have that on my conscience.

Nico bent and kissed my cheek. Sofia walked him to the door, where they exchanged a few hushed words. Before she could shut it behind him, the makeup artists and hairstylists arrived.

Not wanting to worry about anything, I indulged in celebrating with my friends as if everything was normal, as if my wedding had been planned and we'd anticipated this day. Wine flowed. We laughed, drank, and snacked on cheese and fruit as our hair and makeup were done. When the stylists left the room, Sofia helped me into my wedding dress.

None of us said a word for a few seconds as we stood before the mirror. "Sof." I couldn't say anything more. It was beautiful, and I'd never imagined myself at that point, optimistic about my groom. "It's incredible."

She grinned behind me. "It only enhances your beauty." Then she held up two veils for me to choose from. One was simple and would fall in soft folds down my back from the ornate comb it was attached to. The other was a blusher veil that would cover my face, stopping at my chin. I chose the first, wanting to see Max's face clearly.

"I can't believe you're getting married today... and to the hot not-bodyguard," Em mused.

"Me too. But you know we're already married, right?"

"What?" Sofia shrieked then glared when Emiliana didn't have the same response.

Em threw her head back and her throaty laugh surrounded us. "Stefano told me. She got married at the ass crack of dawn."

"That ceremony was in case something happened here and we couldn't complete our vows. This one is Max's gift to me, so that I could have you both here with me."

Sofia took a minute to get her anger under control. "You're lucky we love you so much. Imagine if one of us got married without even a phone call to let you know?" Arms crossed, she jutted her chin out.

"We weren't dressed like this for the wedding. And I didn't have you guys standing up for me. You know it's different."

"Get over it, Sof." Em huffed then went to the closet and took out their dresses.

I guessed the theme was crimson. I could work with that. A

knock sounded then someone said "five minutes" through the closed door.

"I still love you." Sofia gave me a side hug. "And who the hell knows what our weddings will be like?"

I grabbed Sofia's hand before she accepted the floor-length strapless dress Em held out, giving her a squeeze. Emiliana and I shared a look over her head. Enzo would come around.

After Em slipped on her dress and heels, she offered to make sure everything was in place and ready. Thanks to the wine and having my friends with me over the past hour, I wasn't nervous. When she came back in, I couldn't stop myself. "Who's out there?" *Would Antonio Caruso be here to support his son? And what about Tony?*

"Sofia's entire family, mine, Stefano, Eva, loads of cousins, Benito, and a photographer." Em's face was unreadable. "Stefano told me they're posting a picture in the newspaper of your and Max's wedding to get the word out about who he is, so you're even more protected."

"Mm-hmm. Antonio sucks for not acknowledging Max, but maybe he expected that?" I remembered Max mentioning that on the way over. Em worried her lip. I knew why. She'd hesitated over telling me my dad was here. "I'm not upset about Benito." We let that hang out there, none of us wanting to dampen the mood by talking more about him.

"Have you found out Max's story?" Sofia stepped into her dress. When the dress was in place, Emiliana zipped her up.

"I have. It's tragic and will make you despise Antonio and Benito more than you already do." I toyed with the material of my dress. "My grandfather from Sicily sent Max to marry me, to give me protection and a way to escape Benito."

"Are you okay with that? Marrying him?" Em paused in handing me the bouquet of roses that matched their dresses. "What if you find out something you can't live with?"

I shook my head. "No matter what's in his past, he's a better option than Tony. I know my feelings won't change." *Why are the flowers so heavy?* I peered over the top of it then spotted the hilt of a knife. *Nice.*

"Whoa. Feelings?" Em grinned. "What kind? You haven't known Max all that long."

"I don't need to. His actions speak loudly enough. I know I'm married, but he makes me feel free. Protected. Way different than living under Benito's thumb."

Sofia sighed, and Em softened as she opened the door. "Are you happy? I mean truly happy?"

"Things are crazy, and everything is so new, but yes. I am." I squeezed Sofia whose eyes were as suspiciously teary as mine.

"Then let's get out there," she ordered.

I followed them out of the room and down the hallway then paused where Stefano stood at the entrance to the chapel. He opened the door a few inches and signaled to someone inside. When the music started and the voices hushed, he swung the doors wide. Emiliana went first, holding a bouquet of white roses. Then Sofia. Finally, it was my turn.

I paused at the entrance to the cathedral, my pulse pounding against the base of my neck. Benito waited for me, disdain clear in his cold, reproachful gaze and pinched lips. "This wasn't how things were to go. You won't get away with cheating me out of what I should have gained." He growled in my ear as he roughly grabbed my arm. "One way or another, I will make you a widow, back under my control."

It made me wonder if he was the one to tip Tony off about when and where to stage his recent ambush. "You're done." My steady gaze bore into his, and I let him see the truth of my words. "There is nothing you can do to me anymore. Max won't allow it. And honestly, I don't see things ending well for you if you harass me."

Stefano stepped up and murmured into Benito's ear, too quietly for me to hear. But I followed Benito's gaze to the rafters. Cristiano was positioned with his sniper's rifle aimed at my father. Max protected me from all angles, and warmth infused me.

Benito would walk me down the aisle, upholding his part of the contract whether he wanted to or not, because he couldn't risk further destruction of what remained of his empire. I did a quick scan of the guests, noting that Antonio was not present, but his wife, Nicole, was, and I couldn't help but wonder if she was there on her own or as a representative of her husband. From the end of the aisle, my gaze landed on Max. He stood tall, devastatingly handsome in a tailored black suit. It didn't matter what he wore. Nothing could disguise what a powerful force he was. *And he's mine.* My heart stuttered at the flash of admiration and possessiveness I read in his features.

One foot in front of the other, I glided down the aisle, Benito's distant demeanor and grasp on my arm insignificant, my gaze never wavering from Max's face. The photographer continued to capture the moments with us in the cathedral. Our friends and family followed my progress with their eyes, smiles on most of their faces. When I reached Max's side, Benito left without a word, and for that, I was grateful. I handed Sofia my bouquet. Max bent to my ear to whisper, "You're stunning."

Everything around us faded. There was only him. Words were spoken, but I wasn't listening. Instead, all I could think about was the life I would have with him.

I was able to make the appropriate responses when the priest paused, but all I wanted was for Max to kiss me. With a rosary clutched tightly in his hand, the priest had us repeat our vows. Soon after, he pronounced us husband and wife. Then Max's lips were on mine, and everything faded but how he made me feel: both protected and free.

CHAPTER TWENTY-ONE

LILIANA

"How are you doing?" Max's voice carried over the sound of the road as the car sped toward our lakefront home.

"I'm good." I couldn't help the grin that pulled my lips wide. "The ceremony was beautiful and also entertaining, with Tony showing up."

He chuckled, the sound deep and sexy. My fingers curled in my lap to keep my hands to myself when I longed to run them through his dark hair. *Soon.*

"They shouldn't be able to touch you now."

I fidgeted in my seat. One could only hope. I wasn't sure Benito, Antonio, or Tony were on board. "Do you think Antonio sent Tony to try to stop the wedding?"

"I don't really know him, so I can't answer that. He can't change anything now. He'll come to accept his new role."

I wasn't so sure, but I didn't want to waste any more time on Tony.

"I wish we could have had a reception, but my main concern is to make sure you're safe." Max looked at me before returning to watch the road.

"I don't mind about the reception." I was of the same persuasion as Max and wanted to get the heck out of there while things were good.

"We'll go on a honeymoon when things settle down."

His hand rested on my leg, and he gave my thigh a squeeze. A jolt of desire shot straight to my core. We couldn't get home soon enough. I lay my hand over his, intertwining our fingers, my palm against the back of his hand. The contact of skin on skin spiked my heart rate and shot fire through my nerve endings. He flipped his palm then curled his fingers around mine as he pulled into the secure underground parking and shut the car off.

"Wait for me."

I sucked in a breath at the heat blazing in his eyes and nodded, suddenly incapable of forming a coherent response. The way he looked at me like he couldn't wait to get me upstairs made my body tremble.

He released my hand, but the connection that existed between us didn't sever. Energy sizzled between us, and as he opened my door and extended his hand to help me out, the anticipation to be in his arms was almost unbearable.

He drew me close, wrapping an arm around my waist as we stepped into the elevator and rode it to our floor. The doors opened with a swoosh, and we stepped inside our place. Wandering into the main room, I took my veil off then laid it on the back of the couch, loosening my hair so it spilled down my back.

"Do you want anything to drink?" His deep voice sent a shiver racing over my exposed skin. I turned toward him. He'd removed his jacket and was in the process of removing his tie. I crossed the distance between us, murmuring no to a beverage, and helped him take it off. Peering at him from beneath my lashes, I eased the buttons free until the last one was undone.

I leaned in, pressing my lips to the sliver of exposed skin, wanting to touch all of him, to explore every inch of his body.

His heartbeat increased from my touch, and I spread the two halves of his shirt as wide as it would go while the bottom was tucked in, barely holding back a groan at his perfectly sculpted chest before me.

Max drew me closer, crowding me as he found the zipper on my dress and drew it down with agonizing slowness. My breath hitched, heart pounding against my rib cage. There was no mistaking what was on his mind, and I wanted him too.

When he brushed the spaghetti straps from my shoulders, the tight bodice he'd unzipped loosened further. Then the stunning dress pooled to my feet, leaving me in a lace thong.

"You're so beautiful." He drew me to him, and I went willingly. "I want you, Lil. Tell me this is okay."

"Yes." My voice was breathy and heated, and I didn't know what I'd do if he didn't touch me soon. When he cupped the weight of my breast in his palm and rolled the nipple with his fingers, I gasped.

"You have too many clothes on." I tugged at the buttons on his shirt, pulling it from the waistband of his pants until he backed up to tear the clothes from his body.

As his arms slid around me, I trembled. His palm settled on the curve of my spine, and he buried the other in my hair. Then his lips claimed mine, and I opened for him. He deepened the kiss. There was only him. The rest of the world ceased to exist. When he cupped my ass, grinding against my core, I moaned. Heat pooled, and I clenched my thighs together, unsure how much more I could take.

The fabric of my panties tightened then the lacey material fluttered to my feet as he tore them from my body.

Through a haze of desire, I gripped the back of his neck, broke the kiss, then demanded what I needed. "Now Max, don't make me wait."

He backed me into the kitchen with a growl. Then his hands were on my hips, lifting me until I was seated on the island.

Candles flickered, casting a warm glow on his heart-stopping masculinity. I traced the chiseled line of his jaw until the pad of my finger brushed over his lower lip.

With a gentle nudge from his hands, I opened my thighs, baring myself to his hungry gaze. I braced my hands on the cool marble as the pad of his finger traced my slick seam. My head fell back, an unbidden moan falling from my throat. I was more than ready for him. "Hurry."

He shifted, aligning against my core, one hand going to my hip as I wrapped my legs around him. In one thrust, he seated himself fully inside, and I cried out at the fullness. *Heaven.* He held me suspended in that brief moment while I adjusted to the fullness of him. Then he moved, and I was robbed of all thought as the sensations built and my body squeezed him.

The rough scrape of his five-o'clock shadow teased as he dropped his mouth to my neck, grazing his teeth over the sensitive skin as he pumped in and out. My body tightened around him.

He eased back enough and his lips left my neck on a moan. Light from the flickering candles enhanced the sheen of sweat that covered his well-defined shoulders and chest, making me want to touch and lick every inch of him. I writhed against him as he hit that spot deep inside that drove me wild.

With each thrust, I felt our connection solidify and grow stronger. What we had between us was everything.

When he slipped the pad of his thumb between my thighs, applying pressure to my clit, everything escalated. My body clamped around his like a vise, my back arching and the world blinking out of focus. He lifted me from the island, and my legs tightened as he changed the angle.

I screamed as my body exploded with too many sensations, light bursting behind my closed eyelids. One, two thrusts, and he followed me over the edge, riding the wave with me as I went limp in his arms.

His arms tightened around me. After a moment where we clung together, our hearts pounding in sync, he carried me to the bedroom. He laid me on the bed and crawled in next to me, tucking my body against his then pulling the sheet over us. I sighed in contentment. He was home, and I would never let him go.

CHAPTER TWENTY-TWO

LILIANA

I woke to the cry of seagulls and the crashing of waves as they broke along the shore. An occasional horn sounded as traffic sped along Lake Shore Drive. Heat blanketed one side of my body. I rolled onto my back and off Max, who slept beside me. Arching my lower back, I pushed my head into the pillow as I extended my arms overhead until they touched the headboard and languidly stretched.

We were in Max's room—our room. The bed was huge and about the only furniture in there. What I loved the most was the sliding glass door and the attached private balcony with a gorgeous view of Lake Michigan. We'd left the doors open the night before to let the breeze off the lake in and to fall asleep to the sound of the waves. *I could get used to this.*

The bed shifted. Max's hand found my hip and turned me back toward him. We faced one another. "Morning."

"Mmm. Morning." His voice was deep and husky from sleep.

I couldn't stop the grin from pulling my lips wide. He was devastatingly handsome. I gave in to the urge and ran my fingers through his thick, dark hair, loving how mussed it was from sleep. Bringing my hand around to his face, I traced his jaw then ran the pad of my thumb over his sinfully talented lips. The things he'd done to me the night before... my cheeks heated, and my core warmed in response to the sensual memory.

In a slow caress, he explored my body, and I draped my leg over his, letting the intimacy of his touch fill me. With him, I would always want more.

My skin heated beneath his touch. My breath came faster, every nerve ending in my body electrified. He wrapped an arm around me and pulled me close so that our skin touched, and I breathed in his scent, entranced. I trailed kisses over his angular jaw, corded neck, and broad shoulders that flexed as he pleased me. My lower back arched, and I clung to him, a moan thrumming through my throat, ensnaring him into the same trance he had me in.

I'll never get enough of him.

When he stopped his exploration with his hand, my gaze flew to his. Dark promise flashed through his eyes, and then he flipped me onto my back, holding my hands over my head as he bent to my neck. Tilting my head to the side, I gave him better access. The nip of his teeth where my neck and shoulder met sent another wave of desire coursing through my body.

He shoved the sheet away, and I shivered as the cool air caressed my skin. I brought my hands down and trailed them over his broad shoulders, holding his head to me. Another moan escaped my parted lips as he trailed kisses from my neck, over my collarbone, to the valley between my breasts—*this man.*

I'd thought he would be incredible, as I was so in tune with him, but I'd had no idea how amazing we would be together or what he would make me feel.

He cupped my breast, kneading it until I squirmed under him. Heat built, and I tugged at his hair, desperate for him to finish what he'd started. When he lifted his head, obsidian eyes filled with desire met mine.

"Hands above your head."

A jolt of desire slayed me at his guttural words. I complied. When he spread my legs, I whimpered. A slow caress along the inside of my thighs, and I had to fight to keep from lifting my hips. *So close.*

Then his mouth was on me, and his finger eased inside my soaked channel. My head rocked back against the pillow, and I cried out. Another finger joined the first. The friction against my clit made me crazy, and I pushed myself against his mouth, wanting more. Pressure built inside. Everything faded except his touch.

A moan tore from my throat as wave after wave of heightening sensations flooded me. He took me higher, the friction building until I flew over the edge, stars winking behind my eyes.

When he withdrew his mouth and fingers, my heart slowed its frantic pace a bit. Limbs like jelly, I lay there watching his dark head lift. I sucked in a breath at his expression. Naked lust shone in his eyes as he climbed up my body. I cradled him between my legs. The pressure at my entrance had me wantonly rocking against him, needing more. *Always more.* I was quickly becoming an addict where he was concerned.

Then he was pushing inside. My body stretched to accommodate his length and girth. "Give me more," I purred in his ear, tilting my hips to meet his thrust.

His mouth found the corner of my neck, and my nails dug into his back as he growled, burying himself fully, hitting the right spot. My body responded, clenching tightly. The more he moved, the more I lost all sense of time. My skin felt flushed. Then he lifted my knee, changing the angle again.

I cried out as he brought me to the edge again and again, only to slow down before I could fall.

"Goddamn, Lil. I'll never get enough of you," he growled against my skin.

He pulled out, and I groaned in protest. Then he flipped me onto my stomach. His hands grasped my hips, and he pulled me back and up so I was on my knees. "On your elbows."

I complied, my body trembling in anticipation over him entering me again. My fingers gripped the sheet, and my forehead dropped to my fisted hands. With one hand on my hip, anchoring me in place, he flattened the other on the small of my back, arching it and exposing more of me to him.

He lined up at my entrance then seated himself back inside. *So full.* The angle was intense, and I came instantly, my body quivering around him.

He didn't stop. In and out, he kept going and the pressure built again. I cried out as the sensations built to impossible heights until my release exploded with a ferocity that left me shaken. He shouted as he chased my climax with one of his own.

We collapsed together, sweaty and sated. He rolled onto his back and pulled me into his arms. I snuggled against him while he brushed my hair from my face. Content, I tangled my legs with his as the world came back into focus around us. The lakefront breeze swept through our bedroom, cooling our overheated bodies. The rhythmic sound of the waves lulled me into a trancelike state, and I drifted back to sleep in Max's capable embrace.

I wondered if it would always be like that with Max. Sex with him was beyond my wildest imagination. Waking in his arms, I wanted to experience that every day for the rest of my life. He made me feel cherished, loved, and beautiful.

We'd slept most of the morning away then had coffee on the balcony. We spent the remainder of the day in the apartment, just the two of us. Of course, we checked in on Tommasso, who was awake and heavily medicated but on the mend.

The threat from our families remained in the back of our minds, but we refused to let it intrude. In a world were violence and death were the norm for us, we'd learned to cherish the moments we had together because at any given time, hell could and probably would crash down on us.

The day was easy and relaxed. We talked more then made sandwiches together for lunch. As it grew late, he wanted to take me out for dinner. I was all for it.

My phone pinged with a text from Sofia while I was blow-drying my hair. I grinned, shut off the dryer, then leaned a hip against the sink to read her text.

Sofia: *What's it like to be Mrs. Max Caruso?*

Me: *(eye roll emoji) Sounds so formal! Weird. But it's great.*

Sofia: *Happy for you. <3 Invite us over!!*

Me: *Soon. Keeping him to myself for a little longer.*

Sofia: *Any probs w/Tony/Antonio/Benito?*

Me: *No. I think we're good. What can Benito do? He signed the contract. He has no leg to stand on. Tony's pissed, but so long as Antonio doesn't retaliate we should be fine. Since he hasn't... could've at the church.*

Sofia: *Yeah. Had the same thought. Fingers crossed it's all good.*

Me: *Same. Love you!!*

Sofia: *Love you more!*

I set the phone down and finished getting ready. I put my heels on and a pair of diamond earrings then joined Max at the island, where he sipped whiskey.

"You look gorgeous." His eyes sparkled in appreciation. Then he tapped the paper by his elbow. "Our wedding made the paper."

I grinned then sat on the stool beside him. Good thing the photographer was inside when Tony confronted us. That would have been an interesting shot, all of us with our guns out. My gaze skimmed over the image. It was a gorgeous picture. I wanted one to frame. "Did the photographer send you prints?"

"They'll be delivered tomorrow."

I took a minute to skim the article. "You're named as Antonio Caruso's eldest son. Does he know about your public declaration?"

A devilish grin curved Max's lips. "He does now."

I laughed. "Well, then. I guess we'll see how he responds."

"There's not much he can do. It would have made more sense for him to do something before our wedding or even during the ceremony."

"Maybe he's coming to terms with you being a part of his life?"

Max snorted. "I wouldn't go that far." He glanced at the time. "Did you want anything to drink before we leave?"

"No, thanks. Where are we going?" I grabbed my clutch and slipped my phone inside.

"Bramare."

"I love that place. The Vitale family owns it. Enzo took Sofia, Emiliana, and me there a few times." I moved to his side as we walked to the elevator, and his arm went around me, cupping my hip.

We rode the elevator down, got in his Mercedes, and drove the short distance to the restaurant. It didn't take long until we were seated at a secluded table. Max ordered a bottle of wine as we looked over the menu. After making our selections, we both ordered steak, and our waiter uncorked then poured our wine.

When we were alone again, Max reached into his pocket, pulled out a black credit card, and then handed it to me.

"Oh, wow." I peeked up at him and then back to the card. The La Rosa family owned the bank—Sofia's brother Nico worked at the family business—and it would have taken mere minutes to get the card. Judges were also in our pocket, making the rest a snap. "It's strange seeing my new name." *Liliana Caruso* was printed in silver.

"I'm sure it'll take some getting used to."

"Mm-hmm." But not in a bad way.

"What do you think about our lakefront townhome?" Max took a sip of his wine then set it on the table.

"I love it." *Where is he going with this?*

"There are only a few things that I've bought for it so far. If you want to redecorate or make any changes, we can."

I chuckled. He didn't know what he was getting into. "Are you saying you want to be a part of the décor choices or that I should just do whatever I want?"

Our food arrived, smelling heavenly. I hadn't realized how hungry I was.

"I'm curious what you'll choose. Should I be worried?"

I widened my eyes as I chewed then swallowed a bite of asparagus. "Do you not like animal print and mirrors?" At the uncomfortable grimace, I decided to put him out of his misery. "Kidding. I love the blue-gray sheet you have on our bed. The kitchen is perfect. I wouldn't change a thing. That guest room, though."

"Yeah." Mischief flashed in his dark eyes, and his dimple appeared along his right cheek as he laughed. "That room was prepared last minute just for you."

"Lovely. It's got to go."

"I figured. Just no animal print." He winked. "Mirrors in our bedroom could be fun."

I rolled my eyes. "Hard pass." I got the sentiment, and it would have been fun, but mirrors were not my favorite design choice. We chatted about some ideas for our lakefront place and entertained the thought of buying a house closer to the other families. I wouldn't have minded being near Sofia and Emiliana, but being out so far was great too. It was an option, and we would probably have to do it at some point but not immediately.

We were at the table for two hours, and the time flew by. The bottle of wine was replaced by a second. I realized I drank most of the second one and excused myself to the restroom. Max waved for a guard to trail after me. I wanted to argue he wasn't needed but let it go. We were in one of Emiliana's family's restaurants. *What could possibly happen?*

The guard stayed in the hallway not far from the door. I went inside. There was another woman there, drying her hands. After she left, I had the space to myself, but not for long. When I opened the door to go back to the table, Antonio Caruso blocked my path, holding a gun in my face. The guard sent to keep me safe was in a crumpled heap on his left.

Antonio filled the space of the open doorway, soldiers flanking either side of him. He had the same dark hair, gray eyes, and jawline as Max, but where Max's eyes were expressive and warm, Antonio's were cold and dead.

My heart stopped. *Swear to God.* I fumbled with my clutch, trying to get my gun out. He grabbed. I screamed. Then his hand slapped over my mouth, cutting my vocalizations to barely a squeak. I didn't stand a chance. My purse slipped from my hands, the gun inside inaccessible.

Nails digging into Antonio's suit, I struggled. My heel landed against his shin. His grunt shot a surge of satisfaction through me until a small prick at my neck caused the room to spin. My vision tunneled as the drug spread through my system. Then there was nothing but black, and I went limp.

CHAPTER TWENTY-THREE

MAX

Our waitress hurried from where Lil had gone to the restroom, my wife's purse in her hand. The frightened look on her face sent alarm spiraling through me. I met her halfway, gun in hand. My fingers clamped around her arm, and her green eyes went wide. "Where's my wife?"

The purse was between us, and I let go of her to take it. Tears streamed down the terrified waitress's cheeks as she stuttered, "Y-Y-Your father carried her o-out the back."

Christ. I had to be sure, though. "How do you know he's my father?"

"S-S-Scar over his left eyebrow. Antonio Caruso. Looks like you but older."

That was all I needed to hear. Fury spread through me as I raced to where she'd pointed. The guard lay on the ground in a pool of blood. Slamming through the back door, my gaze darted around the employee parking lot. She was gone. There was no trace of her. A sense of fear and devastation threatened to override my anger, but I couldn't let it. I needed to stay focused, driven, until she was safely in my arms. And she would be. *Antonio will not win.*

Too many minutes later, I was in my car and racing toward Antonio's house, having already informed Sal and Cristiano, who were en route. Tommasso was on his feet but in pain. He would guard the house and call if she returned.

It was time I called in allies, as many of the branches of the five families as I could. I needed a show of force.

After my cousins, I put a brief call in to Vincenzo Brambilla, who was in Italy and just as furious. The jet would be fired up within the hour, along with fifteen passengers. It was time to act, sooner than I'd thought, but Antonio had gone too far.

Through my Bluetooth, I connected to Stefano's cell, waiting for him to pick up. *Come on.* I was barely holding it together. My knuckles were white on the steering wheel. Weaving in and out of cars, I pushed the pedal to the floor. Thanks to Stefano orchestrating the press and the wedding article announcement, the cops knew who I was and what my car looked like. They would not stop me. We owned this city.

"What?" Stefano snapped.

I didn't care what I'd interrupted. He was often in a shitty mood, anyway. "Antonio took Liliana from Bramare. The waitress said she was unconscious, so likely drugged."

"Fuck."

Exactly. "I need the families behind me on this. A show of force. Of support. Antonio needs to feel like an island without a bridge to the mainland."

"La Rosa and Vitale will come for blood."

"Benito won't support Lil." The car careened around a corner, fishtailing before I got it back in control.

"I may be able to get Frank on board because he hates Benito."

"And since she told me that Benito hates Frank, his support would be a slap in the face to him."

"Fuck," Stefano said again. "Okay. On it."

There was more I had to tell him. He needed to be prepared

and warn the others. "I called a commission. The Sicilians will be here day after tomorrow."

"This should be interesting. I can almost promise you'll have Frank on your side for this."

"I need you to inform the families. I'm almost at Antonio's house."

"Hold up. I'm on my way. I'll call them from the car."

I grunted my response.

"Don't go in. Wait for me."

"Why would I do that?" His house was in sight. Soldiers were patrolling—a lot of them.

"Because you can't kill him. And I know you want to."

He was right. Reluctantly, I pulled to the side of the road. Antonio's made men faced me from their positions at the end of the drive, guns at the ready.

Stefano better bring more ammo. I had a 9mm and an extra magazine on me. I had a lockbox in the car with an automatic and more ammunition, but we could always use more.

My mind ticked through scenarios that caused my gut to churn with a barely contained murderous rage. Liliana had come to mean everything to me. She stopped being a pawn in my plan almost from the start. From there, my feelings had only grown, and I didn't want to live without her. *God help Antonio.* If he did anything to her, he would wish he was dead after I finished with him.

A handful of minutes ticked by before a black SUV screeched to a stop behind me. Then Stefano was out and at my door. I got out, tapping my gun at the side of my leg. Tense, I wanted to start shooting.

"We'll take my car." Stefano's steady gaze held mine. He got in my face. "Do not kill Antonio."

Satisfaction burned in me. He didn't say not to shoot him. No reason I couldn't spill his blood a little... or a lot.

As he turned to get into his SUV, I pivoted and shot the

soldiers with their guns trained on us at the end of the drive-way. Antonio needed a message other than our little face-to-face visit.

Stefano stopped, shot me an annoyed look, then got behind the wheel. "Antonio already knows we're here."

I grunted. Didn't matter. There would be four fewer guards in our way when we left. "We need a plan." From what I knew about Antonio, taking Lil was about control and vengeance. He wouldn't want me to take over Tony's position, especially as he didn't have any influence over me. Tony, he'd raised. I was a wildcard.

Stefano gunned the engine, and we flew up the long drive-way. By the time we screeched to a stop in front of the door, more men had surrounded the entrance. One stepped forward as we got out. Both hands were raised and in one, he clutched a cell phone with the screen lit. None of the other soldiers touched their weapons.

"Boss isn't here," the guard with the phone stated. "He's on the phone."

I took the phone from him and put it to my ear, then growled. "Where the fuck is she?"

A dark, twisted chuckle was my reply, and if he had been there, I would have enjoyed shooting him several times, rules be damned. He'd taken my heart.

"If you hurt her in any way, know that I'll take everything you care about from you. I won't kill you. Not until you've lost everything. Then, you'll wish I'd pulled the trigger from the pain of what else I'll do."

"You won't do a goddamned thing." Antonio's voice was measured, controlled. "We will come to an agreement about your involvement in my business. Which will be exactly zero. You're not a Caruso. I renounced you when I left you to die in that hospital in Italy. If you want Liliana back, then you'll agree to my terms. You have twelve hours to make a decision. If you don't, I'll send you piece by piece of her until you do." The line went dead.

My hand tightened on my phone until a crack sounded in my ear. I forced myself to relax then tossed it to the guard. "Tell Nicole to come out here."

"She's not home either," the same soldier answered.

Without a word, I got in the passenger seat, and Stefano followed. Not one of Antonio's soldiers moved or went for their weapons. I sent a text to Sal that we were leaving and for him and Cris to go back home for now.

It bothered me that Nicole wasn't there. More questions were raised in her absence. I was at that dinner and had seen how her husband and son treated her, and the way Lil had stood up for her then got her away from them. Nicole liked Lil—I could see it in the way her shoulders relaxed and her smile reflected in her eyes around her. Wherever she was, I hoped that she would help Lil.

It was information I stored away but had little time to ponder.

The weight of my gun was the only thing holding me together. With it, I would make Antonio suffer. I had one option, only one, really, to save Liliana from the torture Antonio planned.

I half turned in my seat. "Where's Tony?"

I needed to find my half-brother, and when I did, Antonio wouldn't lay a hand on Liliana.

Liliana

I woke nauseous and with a pounding headache. Confusion swirled through my mind. *Did I drink too much?* I lay still, breathing through the worst of the dizziness, cataloging what I could. It was quiet. I couldn't detect anyone else where I was. No sound of the lake. Maybe a fan whirling. It was hard to tell. There was nothing soft about where I was lying. *Did I fall out of bed, or am I in the bathroom?*

My fingers twitched but found no purchase. There were no blankets. Under the pads of my fingers was rough wood, possibly unfinished. My instincts flared, and I forced myself to relax, to appear as if I was sleeping as the events rolled through my disoriented brain.

I wasn't at home. I'd never returned from the restaurant. *Max!* He must have been out of his mind with worry. I peeled my eyelids open, and they scratched my dry eyes like sandpaper. *Did something die in my mouth? Ugh.*

A convulsion rocked my body, curving my shoulders in. I drew my knees up when it passed. I took a few slow breaths, ensuring I wasn't going to throw up while I thought about the last thing I remembered.

Antonio. Dread swept over me as I lay on the floor. *Is he here?* My gaze darted around the dark space. The scent of dust and mold was thick in the stale air. Confident I was alone, I felt for the sheath around my thigh where I had a weapon. Unsurprisingly, it was gone. Sadly, my gun was back in the restaurant on the floor. I hoped Max understood what had happened to me. Antonio would pay for what he'd done, I had no doubt. As it was, Max wanted blood for how he'd abandoned him, leaving him for dead. If not for his mother's family coming to his aid, things would have been bleak.

Time to get out of here. I was no damsel in distress, and I wasn't tied up. That gave me an advantage. Fighting through the drug's symptoms, I pushed to my feet, wavering until I got control of my weakened muscles.

My feet were bare. The heels must have fallen off when Antonio carried me from the restaurant. Maybe Max found those too. All I could make out in the cramped space were what looked like boxes and some furniture. With care, I moved closer. As I crossed to the other side, where a couple of chairs were stacked, I stepped on a board that squeaked. Frozen, I waited to see if that had alerted whoever was below the attic. There had to have been someone there.

I needed a weapon. There had to be something in one of the boxes. I turned to the closest one then tore the tape off. When I felt inside, I found books, but anything could be used as a weapon. Mentally, I added that to my hopefully building arsenal.

Not even five minutes later, I heard the groan of what had to be the stairs lowered to access the attic. When the hatch flipped open, I whirled around, book in hand, to find Antonio's wife, Nicole, framed in the light from below. She cackled when she noticed what I was holding. It was no match for the gun aimed at me.

CHAPTER TWENTY-FOUR

MAX

Stefano and I parked at Envy, a club owned by Enzo Vitale. Emiliana, Enzo's sister and Lil's friend, had called with information that Tony had been spotted inside. There was a line out the door and around the block to get in. At almost midnight, it was unlikely that most of them would. Bouncers manned the door. Occasionally, one of them would walk the line, pick a few people, and usher them inside.

When the door opened, the deep bass and conversation would spill outside and through our open windows. I palmed my gun, unwilling to put it away. We waited in the car for Enzo to come out and give us information about where Tony was inside. There were several floors and private sections where VIPs would entertain friends, which was likely where he was. We needed to know to maintain the element of surprise.

Because Tony was coming with me—he was my insurance against Lil being harmed.

"There he is."

I spotted Enzo coming out of the front as Stefano pointed him out. About my height, he walked as if he could handle himself. He said something to the bouncer then headed for our car. I studied his face, noting the similarities to Em with his dark hair and eyes, along with their high cheekbones. When he got to the window, I didn't care about the family resemblance, just the details I needed.

"Where is Tony?"

"You should know that the girls are here. They wanted in on the plan and are making sure Tony stays put. Do not hurt them."

"Sofia and Emiliana?"

Enzo gave a curt nod.

"I have no reason to harm them, and Lil would crucify me if I did. Not the goal."

With a nod to Stefano, Enzo asked, "How's this going down?"

Stefano snorted. "It's his show. He'll go in and bring Tony out. I'll be out back. Just clear anyone from the back exit."

Enzo tapped on the roof of the car. "Already done. Come with me, and I'll lead you to the private room he's in."

That's all I needed. I pushed the door open as Enzo moved out of the way. As soon as I was clear, Stefano took off for the back entrance. He waited until I walked beside him. I would've done the same. Trust didn't come easy to any of us.

Once inside the dimly lit club, people and heart-thumping music surrounded us. It didn't last long before he took me through the main floor and to the back, where the music wasn't as loud.

"Lil's important not just to the girls but to the rest of us as well." Enzo talked as he led us through a hallway then to a private elevator. "We're not like the bosses. Not all of them, anyway."

I grunted a noncommittal response. While I would have wanted that information under normal circumstances, nothing about what was happening was normal. *Find Tony. Force Antonio's hand. Save Lil.* It was difficult to focus past the red tunnel vision.

Enzo's steady gaze met mine. "Stefano filled us in a little about who you are and what happened. When we get Liliana back, we need to sit down and figure a few things out."

That would happen sooner than he thought. "A commission has been called."

Enzo turned toward me as the elevator doors opened. His brows rose, and he waited for a beat before indicating which direction we would go. "Goddamn, you work fast. All right. I'm on board to shake up the families." He reached around and under his suit jacket, pulled out a Glock, then opened the door in front of where we stood.

When he pushed it open, neither of us moved for several seconds at the sight before us. He hadn't been kidding about Sofia and Emiliana wanting to help. Tony was inside the spacious room with a view from one side to the dance floor a couple levels below, tied to a chair. Emiliana and Sofia stood over him. There were several long cuts along his forearms and one on his neck, but none were deep. The glazed look in my half-brother's eyes told me that the girls might have given him the truth serum that they'd told Lil to use when she got Tony alone.

Enzo's deep laughter pulled me from the stupor I was stuck in. It stopped when Sofia moved her hand, a syringe dangling from her fingers.

"Looks like you did some of the work for me." I let a menacing grin curve my mouth. I wanted Tony to know we weren't there to save him but to deliver our brand of torture.

"What was in that?" Tony growled. "It better have come from Trey."

Defiance flashed in Sofia's gaze, and she jutted out her chin at Enzo. A second passed before she tossed the syringe on the table. "You're going to question me? Really? It's like you don't even know me."

"We're not done." Em's full red lips were pressed tightly

AMY MCKINLEY

together, and she alternated a glare between Enzo and me. "He says he knows nothing about where Lil is. That may be true. His dad told him to stay where he'll have witnesses and not to leave until the place closed. Seems he slipped his guards and defied his dad. This wasn't where he was supposed to go. Bet your regretting that about now, huh, Tony?" Em smacked the side of his head before turning back to us. "When we question him about Marissa, he's just confused." She vibrated with fury. "We need to work him over some more. Hand me your gun." With her hand held out, she motioned for Enzo to give it over.

"Where the hell is yours?" Enzo roared. "You're not to leave the goddamned house without it. You know this."

"I was in a rush and switched purses. It wasn't intentional," she snapped.

"Then you need to have one in every purse you own." Enzo looked like he was about to snap. "You're usually an arsenal when you leave the house. I swear, Em, if you even think about going anywhere without—"

A knife thunked in the doorframe behind us, narrowly missing Enzo's ear.

"That's more like it." Pride flashed in his eyes. Then he turned to Sofia. "You'd better have a gun."

When she slipped off her jacket and turned, Stefano stepped in front of me, blocking my view of the opened-back shirt she wore. Interesting, but I didn't have time for their flirting.

"As entertaining as this is"—I included all of them—"we have work to do." I took out my phone then met their gazes. "Not a word."

Tony's head had lolled back. He looked close to passing out. Truth serum could make the person injected with it groggy and more susceptible to revealing things, but it wasn't a magic drug that forced the person under its influence to tell the truth.

I pulled out my phone and pressed the connection for Antonio. It rang several times until he answered.

"Ready to deal? Or am I sending the first body part?"

Em choked, and I shot a glare her way.

"I'm ready to deal, but not in the way you expect." Closing the distance to Tony, I grabbed the hair on the top of his head and forced his glassy eyes to meet mine. "I have Tony here with me." I shook his head. "Say hi to your father."

"Hey, Pops," Tony slurred, and Antonio went silent.

"Let me make myself clear. If you harm any part of Lil, mentally or physically, I will do the same to Tony but ten times over. Just so that you understand, if you cut off even the tip of Lil's finger, Tony here will lose his right hand."

"What do you want?" Antonio said with a growl.

"I want Liliana returned to me in the same condition she was in before you took her. And I suggest you do so immediately. This isn't going to look good for you to the commission that's happening soon."

With that, I disconnected the call then knocked Tony out with the butt of my gun. When Tony's bindings were cut, I hefted him over my shoulder. We were done there. The second chess piece had been moved. Now, we waited.

"Where are you taking him?" Sofia asked as she stood next to Enzo.

"Back to my place."

"We're coming with," Enzo said for all of them. "Sofia's brothers will meet us there, but we're all a part of this, and there are things we need to resolve before the commission meets."

Liliana

I peered at Nicole's hand through the dark attic, trying to determine if her finger was on the trigger. She looked like she'd already had a few drinks. All it would take was one trip or stumble, and the gun would go off, more than likely hitting me with a bullet. I didn't dare say a word. I wasn't sure what she had planned but caught a glimpse of more of her as she juggled two glasses and a stun gun in one hand, a bottle of grappa tucked in the crook of her elbow.

My brows rose as she somehow managed to climb the rest of the ladder, step onto the plank floor, and cross the distance so there was only a couple of feet left between us. She set the grappa and glasses on the floor then sat across from me. The entire time, her gun remained roughly on me. She wasn't the steadiest person.

"Hey, sweetie." She gave me a half-hearted smile. "I hate to be the one to detain you, as you've always been nice to me. Can't say the same for everyone else, though." She waved away her random thought with a manicured hand. "You've been sleeping for three hours. It's almost midnight, and I'm bored out of my mind. Since we're both stuck here, I thought we could at least enjoy ourselves."

"Why are you doing this?" I needed more answers. Overpowering her wouldn't be too hard as long as she moved the angle of the gun. But she liked me, and there was a small chance she would let me go.

"I'm not doing it. Antonio is. And what he wants, he gets. By the way"—she splashed grappa into two glasses then handed me one—"did you know how much he hates your father? Whew, I've heard so many rants. Benito this, Benito that. Make him pay. Blah, blah, blah."

"So he's holding me because of how much he hates my father?" Highly doubtful.

"No, sorry about that. Went off on a tangent." She pushed

some hair from her face then traded the gun for her Taser. The gun was secure in her lap, still pointed at me for easy grasp.

While she might have missed with the gun, the Taser would be easier. I bet she had my knife too. I sighed and picked up my drink, mentally settling in. "You were saying?"

"Antonio is making both of us stay here… well, me to watch you… because of Max. He doesn't trust him. I can't say I blame him. I mean, Max just showed up." She took a sip then went for a gulp. "And he wants what's rightfully Tony's. Not gonna happen."

"Why are we here? What's Antonio going to do?" Maybe if I included her in my plight, she would think she, too, was being punished. She kind of was if he stuck her as my babysitter. "Are there soldiers keeping us here?"

"Oh, honey." Her Botox-frozen face never betrayed the heavy sarcasm in her voice. "I couldn't tell you what that man will do from one moment to the next. While we're here, we may as well enjoy ourselves."

I lifted my glass, clinked the edge of hers, then took a sip.

She shuddered after her drink. "I hate this place."

"Where are we?" I asked again.

"It's a cottage off the beaten path that no one will ever find. Been in my family forever. They're all dead now, and Antonio likes to use it from time to time for situations like what you're in."

I shifted, and she seemed to read my intent immediately.

Nicole might have been a social climber and an alcoholic, but she was shrewd and smart, something many people missed. She landed Antonio, after all. That said something. "I'm not going to shoot you. Not my way, and as I said earlier, I like you. But I won't cross Antonio. Things won't end well if I do. So even if you manage to overpower me, which won't happen because of this"—she waved the Taser in front of me—"the

guards out front will stop you, and where we are, this place...
help won't be coming. It's untraceable."

I'm screwed. As each minute passed and the drug's grip on my
mind and body loosened a little more, fear took its place. My
teeth sunk into my bottom lip, and I tasted blood. *No one knows
where I am.* Max wouldn't be able to find me, and even if Nicole
wouldn't do anything to harm me, Antonio would.

CHAPTER TWENTY-FIVE

MAX

E xhaustion should have hit from being up all night. It
hadn't. A constant influx of adrenaline fueled my worry
about Lil. I had to believe that Antonio wouldn't lay a hand on
her for fear that I would do so much worse to his son.

Liliana was a fighter. I hoped she would find a way to free
herself or manipulate the situation if needed. The worst-case
scenario wasn't even an option to contemplate.

I rounded to the back of the SUV with Tony's heavy body
over my shoulder. Stefano opened the rear door, and after I
threw Tony in, we took off, heading to my place. We hit a bump,
and Tony's incessant snoring hiccuped, only to start up even
louder. The little I'd learned about my half-brother hadn't
impressed me.

I kept a lookout for possible trouble if Antonio sent men to
stop us from leaving the club, as my guess was that he knew
where his son had gone. When I glanced in the side mirror, it
was to see another car following. "Enzo?"

Stefano grinned. "You didn't think he would wait until you
were ready to talk, did you? The girls are with him too."

Great, so much for keeping my place a secret. I gave Stefano the address, but the smirk told me he already knew it. "How long?"

"Since you and your cousins came to town."

I shook my head. It was the only thing I could do. If Stefano or anyone who needed watching stepped off a plane in Italy, I would have done the same. Fortunately, we'd built a level of trust years ago after I'd helped him rescue Emiliana.

Enough. I couldn't go there, not with Lil out of my reach. I glanced at the back, where Tony was oblivious to what was happening. I had no feelings for my brother. We didn't know each other. He was a means to an end, and I hoped with everything in me that it would be a safe one.

Stefano pulled up to the underground parking garage, and I pressed in a code to make the door go up. Enzo was on our tail with Emiliana and Sofia and followed us inside. I sent a text to Sal, who would tell Tommasso and Cristiano that we were on our way up. Since my floor was set up with the locked bedroom door, that's where we were headed. We packed into the elevator and rose to the top. I went straight to the spare room and dropped Tony on the bed. Next, I stripped him down to his boxers, took everything out with me, then bolted the door behind me, effectively securing him inside.

Back in the living room and kitchen area, I went to the liquor cabinet and got out a couple of whiskey bottles. As I set glasses on the island, my cousins got off the elevator. Tommasso's swollen face was slightly better. His eyes were open, and he was moving around better.

There was an air of expectancy in the room. I scrubbed my hands over my face, hating how helpless I felt.

"So," Sofia circled the open space. "This is where you took our girl. Nice place. You own the building?"

When I nodded, Emiliana laughed. "Better make sure there's a floor for us. We'll be here now and again."

"Yep." Sofia popped the p. "We're a package deal."

Enzo scowled, and Sofia slapped his shoulder. "Not like that, perv."

"That's not what I was thinking," he grumbled. "You're a handful as it is. I don't wish the three of you on my worst enemy. Case in point, what we walked in on earlier this evening with the two of you and Tony."

"Please." She rolled her eyes, fell onto one of the armchairs, then crossed her legs. "It was nothing, and you know it." When her phone pinged from an incoming text, she glanced at it then waved at me. "My brothers are here. Let them up."

Right. Trey had been there to patch up my cousin. I pressed the code to let them in through the street entrance. Once they were in the elevator, I gave them access.

We waited for the doors to open, and in walked Sofia's brothers: Marco, Nico, and Trey. Three of the siblings shared the same shade of dark-brown hair and amber-colored eyes, except Marco, who had black hair and green eyes.

"Let's talk about why we're all here." Stefano poured several shots of whiskey, handing one to Emiliana then one to Sofia. "What do you plan to accomplish with the commission?"

"You called in the Sicilians." Enzo groaned. "Just what type of bloodshed are you expecting? Your own? Ours? I want to be prepared here." He downed his shot. "And before you say anything"—his eyes went cold, the assassin in him coming to the forefront—"I've got your back on this. Lil's ours, and no one hurts the ones we love and gets away with it."

I could sense the closeness between the people in the room, something that went beyond Mafia. "This is what we need to accomplish with the five families, trust and working together, not the disloyalty that's present with some of the older bosses. Times are changing. When we get Lil back safely we need to usher in a new era of ruling." *Starting with taking Antonio out of the running.*

Stefano grunted his agreement then tossed his drink back.

When Emiliana sat on the stool next to him, he braced his hand on the back of her chair and the other on the island, surrounding her. The tension bracketing her mouth eased, and she leaned back to where his hand was.

There were nods at what I'd said, but we needed to focus on other things for the time being. "The commission was called because Antonio took my wife with intent to harm or kill her if I didn't step down from my demands to assume Tony's position."

"Are you aware of the Sicilians' position on your claim that you're Antonio's eldest son?" Marco asked as he took one of the whiskeys already poured.

I nodded. "Vincenzo Brambilla is aware of everything."

"Our parents"—Marco gestured at Enzo—"will meet their jet and accompany them to the north side warehouse."

"Then we better go over what we expect to happen as well as what could go wrong." Stefano had confirmed his father, Frank Rossi, would be in attendance, but we didn't know about Benito and Antonio. Tony would be absent. Emiliana and Sofia were left behind and were given the key in the spare room to extract information from Tony.

"It's simple." I got to the heart of the reason for the commission. "I need to gain power through the commission's vote to take out Antonio when we rescue Lil. Once I'm boss, there will be no more threats from Benito or Tony."

"They're not going to stop just because you're boss," Sofia interjected.

"True, but I'll have the power to handle Tony as I see fit. Benito is another issue that will have to be dealt with."

"You think you'll be boss for both families?" Enzo's brows rose in challenge.

I shook my head. I didn't want that. "That's not the issue yet, and no, I won't."

"And if we can't get to Lil? We don't know where she is."

Stefano's question chilled me to the bone. "We need to track Antonio hard. He'll eventually lead us to her."

Stefano turned to Nico. "That would be you."

Nico nodded. "I'm on it. I need a laptop."

I met Sal's gaze, and he went into my room and retrieved it then gave it to Nico so he could get started.

It was time to lay out the worst-case scenario part of my plan. "If the commission doesn't give me permission, I will still go after Antonio with everything I've got." I wouldn't leave anything to chance, not with Lil's life in the balance.

When it was time, Stefano, Enzo, and I piled into our cars and drove to where the commission would be held. By design, the warehouse all five families owned at the edge of Chicago's north side didn't have any windows. What happened inside stayed within those metal walls. The cement floors were stained with blood. The families held commissions there, fealty was sworn as men became made under new Mafia bosses, and judgment was enacted.

The sleeves of my wrinkled white button-down were rolled up to my forearms, the collar open. I wasn't there to make a good impression for a face-to-face with the other Mafia bosses, so I hadn't bothered with my suit jacket. My cousins and I waited with the group that had crowded my lakefront home a few hours before. I trusted Stefano and hoped to forge ironclad ties with the rest of the Italian-Americans. None of them were happy that the Sicilians had been called in. Bloodshed was likely, but that would be later, when I found Antonio and his followers.

This meeting was a formality to give me the permission I sought to end Antonio and take over as boss—the final part of my plan.

There were no windows inside the cavernous structure, but I knew the hour was getting late, that the sun was near setting. When the door opened, we reacted and aimed our guns at the entrance where Frank Rossi stood with Drago, his advisor. A smirk curved Frank's mouth, only accenting his strong jaw. The resemblance between the two men was eerie. Frank was an older version of Stefano, both with chiseled features, dark eyes that spoke of death, and a ruthless air emanating from their solid six-foot-plus frames.

A scar bisected one side of Drago's face from cheek to chin, adding character to his plain features. I didn't have as much intel on him as I would have liked, but as far as I could tell, his loyalty extended to Frank's underboss and son, Stefano.

The question was whether Benito Brambilla would show. Antonio Caruso would not. That would have been suicide. I would kill him immediately after I got the information about where he was holding Liliana. The bad blood between us went too deep for reconciliation, and torturing him was in the forefront of my thoughts.

Frank and Drago took position near the door where the Sicilians would enter. We didn't have long to wait. Not even ten minutes later, Enzo checked a text, his face grim. "They're here." His voice sliced through the murmurs, silencing them.

Two minutes later, the door opened, and in came the five Sicilian bosses, their underbosses, advisors, and the Italian-American bosses Emilio Vitale and Roberto La Rosa.

The associates fanned around a large table. Once the heads of the families were seated, the meeting began. As I'd called the meeting, I took Antonio Caruso's place, which would also set the tone for what needed to happen.

"Thank you for coming." I addressed each of the men, pausing on Vincenzo Brambilla. "As you may know from my conversation with Vincenzo about his granddaughter, Liliana, my wife, was taken Sunday night by Antonio Caruso, my father.

He's threatened to send pieces of her to me if I don't relent on my claim as a functioning member of the Caruso family."

"He must be stopped!" Vincenzo yelled, his fist coming down on the table with a thud, "by whatever means." Noises of agreement went around the table.

"I'm holding his son Tony captive in an attempt to still Antonio's hand from harming her."

"We agree," Vincenzo said, and the other bosses all gave their acknowledgment.

Mario, the head of the Sicilian Caruso family, held up his palm, and the room went silent. "Tony is the underboss. What was the position in the family that you were to assume as the eldest prodigal son?"

"Second-in-command. Underboss."

"And Antonio's decision on the position?" Mario prodded.

"He is against it. Tony, however, will relinquish his role, moving down in rank."

"I have met Tony as well as having the pleasure of knowing you as you've grown and the man you've become," Mario said. "Vincenzo has argued on your and Liliana's behalf, and the injustices done, on the trip here. I agree with the new ranking order. As underboss to the Italian-American Caruso family, you are well within your right to proceed as acting boss in Antonio's absence, at least until Liliana is returned to you and Antonio is no longer in hiding."

The meeting progressed quickly from that point. Before we dispersed, Vincenzo approached me, and we moved away from the rest so we could speak in private.

"You will bring Liliana home by whatever means necessary. Quickly," he said with an authority that made my spine straighten. He was a man I'd looked up to for more years than I could count.

"You have my word."

Vincenzo's hand landed on my shoulder in a strong grip.

"We will remain until she returns and you are sworn in." He paused, making sure his insinuation was clear. "I would like time with my granddaughter before I fly home."

I nodded. We were on the same bloody page. Antonio's days as boss were numbered.

CHAPTER TWENTY-SIX

LILITANA

"Are you sure it's okay to mix alcohol with whatever Antonio gave me?" My head spun, and I had to squint to see the hand of cards I held.

Nicole snorted. "Doll, I've popped enough pills and chased them with harder stuff than we're drinking. You'll be fine." She picked up a book from the box next to us then threw it at the floor near her feet with a viciousness that made me jump.

A shot of adrenaline coursed through me from the noise, and with it, a little soberness. "What the hell was that about?"

"Spiders." She sneered. "Have I told you how much I hate this place? It's nothing but bad memories. Rats, bugs, not enough food. And don't get me started on my lousy parents."

"You grew up here?" I took a sip, relishing the burn as it went down, then gave the tiny attic another visual sweep. We'd taken two of the wooden chairs and flipped them over. Between us was an overturned box that we used to play cards, which Nicole had found when she'd rummaged through one of the boxes. She'd turned on a pull-cord light bulb hanging from the ceiling that I hadn't noticed when I'd first come to. The space was small and filthy. I understood why she hated it there.

"How did you meet Antonio if you grew up—"

"Poor?" Nicole snorted again. "Oh, honey, I had my sights set on him for a long time. A friend and I went to Envy one night. Her family wasn't as bad off, and she'd loaned me some clothes. I had a fake ID, wasn't quite twenty-one. Eighteen, actually. Didn't matter. I was determined to get out of that life, and we'd heard the Mafia sometimes went to that club. He was there that night. The rest wasn't hard."

I nodded, processing as much as my muddied thoughts would allow. "No offense, but Antonio's an asshole."

She waved my comment away. "None taken. But his money is glorious."

Again, my gaze swept the dilapidated structure we were in. She wasn't wrong. "And what about Max coming into the picture? Does that cause a problem for you?"

"For me? No. But for Tony." She shrugged, sorrow pulling her lips into a frown. "He's a man now and needs to figure things out on his own. Don't get me wrong... I don't like that my son will lose out."

My brows rose.

She pursed her overly full lips. "I can see the writing on the wall, even if Tony can't. Max has that killer drive. Tony is still a baby in that regard. He's too spoiled, has had everything handed to him." She shook her head. "Antonio tied my hands. I feel like I lost Tony a long time ago. If he'd even had a year or two with my family, they would have beaten that part out. Then he would be ready to do what he needs to when it comes time to be boss."

Chills danced over my skin. I needed to gauge what was happening a little better. I knew I could get past her, but the number of guards outside would be a problem even with a Taser. "When do you expect Antonio? What is he going to do to me?"

"Doll, do you really want to know that?" Her big eyes swam with sympathy.

Maybe I can bribe her to let me go. "What would it take for you to release me?"

She set her cards down, her gaze surprisingly steady on mine, given the amount of whiskey we'd consumed. "I don't want you to be hurt, and I'll do everything I can to help you. But there are some things with Antonio that I can't cross. I'm as much of a prisoner here as you are. The guards were instructed to keep us both inside. If we attempt to escape they will shoot us, not to kill but... we might wish for that."

"This life..."

"I know. It's not the easiest. When I met Antonio, he was still grieving for Max's mother." She pursed her lips, her head tilting to the side. "You know I've had a lot of work done."

Uncomfortable, I offered a slight nod, my gaze never straying from hers.

"The thing with people who go under the knife is we can always spot another. Benito's had work done. Why do you think that is?"

Whoa, that was news to me. "I have no idea."

"Antonio hates him. And you know my personality." I grinned along with her. "I pushed and prodded when the situation was right and I found out why. It's not a good story, but you should know it."

I leaned forward, greedy for anything she would share.

"Benito killed Maria, Antonio's first wife, and cost him a son. I'm sorry to say that Maria was retaliation, and you were supposed to be too."

"Oh, God." I felt sick. Max had told me Benito gave his mom the keys to the car when they were in Italy, but there was no driver. He'd suspected Benito had something to do with the crash. Nicole had just confirmed it. "My father is evil."

"He's not the only one. My husband matches him in that department." She shook her head. "I'm sorry you're in this situation. If we could get out right now without retribution, I would do it. But honey, you know they'll come for us, and when they find us, it won't be pretty."

Max

After the commission, Stefano, Enzo, and I returned to my home. They remained in the car while I went up to check on a few things. Between the three of us, we had enough ammo for a full-blown war. Too much deliberation had gone on before we were able to get away from the commission. Having the other bosses and even Vincenzo Brambilla there wasn't the way we wanted to handle things, but it had been necessary. I planned on ending Antonio. It was my right.

Nico had tried to trace Antonio's phone, his credit cards, then hack his GPS, but he'd prepared. He'd even checked cameras around the city. Antonio's cars were all accounted for, phone off and untraceable. He undoubtedly had another car no one knew about. Vito, his advisor, wasn't accessible, either. Nicole's phone was at home, but the girls had helped and forced Tony to call her with the threat of removing a finger if he even hinted something was wrong. When Nicole didn't answer, he asked to speak to the head of their staff to see if she was home. She'd left soon after Liliana was taken from the restaurant and hadn't returned since.

We had to work under the assumption that they were using burners.

Other than that, Tony wasn't much help. While we were holding him in the spare bedroom in my lakefront home, Emiliana and Sofia had tortured him, but they were back in the kitchen, catching up on what had happened with the commission. They would stay back with my cousin in case Tony happened to remember something about where his father may have taken Lil.

One thing was for certain. What happened next would drive an irreparable wedge between Tony and me.

Before I knew it, I was in front of the guest room where he was under lock and key, which wasn't what I wanted. I would give him one last chance, and if he didn't show me anything worthy of salvaging, I would cut him from my heart for good.

The bolt slid back as I unlocked the door. I schooled my features into indifference as I entered the room. Tony was bound at his hands and feet and sitting with his back to the headboard. It wasn't the worst captive situation.

"What do you hope to accomplish?" A light-brown eyebrow arced over dark eyes that flashed hatred, his lips lifted in a smirk. "Father to accept you? A position within our organization?"

"I don't have to hope for anything. I'm coming from the commission, where as the eldest son, I was named acting boss by the Sicilians while Antonio is MIA and holding my wife."

"That isn't possible. You're not the underboss." Red infused his face. "That position is mine."

The Sicilian bosses weren't wrong in their assessment of Tony. He had a lot of growing up to do. He spent too much time partying and doing the bare minimum, while Antonio preferred to maintain control of everything. My guess was that Tony was rarely brought into the decisions. "This is your only chance to prove to me that you're worth a position of importance in the Caruso organization. Where would Antonio take Liliana?"

Laughter spilled from his lips. When he got himself under control, he shook his head mockingly. "It's too bad you don't know my father well enough to anticipate where he would go. Looks like you lost out. When he's done with her, everything will return to how it should be."

I didn't waste any more time. We were done. I left the room, relocked the door, then dropped the key into Emiliana's outstretched palm. Not far from the doorway, she had been leaning against the wall, listening.

"He's not like the rest of us," she said. "We live and breathe this world. Tony was allowed to exist in a position not too dissimilar from his mother's. He's Antonio's heir but not taken seriously. You should know he was groomed in Antonio's image as a cruel and heartless monster, a psychopath."

I nodded, acknowledging her assessment. "I'll call when we have Lil."

Tears misted her eyes, and her fingers curled around the key. "Please do."

Stefano and Enzo were waiting for me in the garage. We took two cars and went to Antonio's house first to see if we could get any information from Nicole or the guards.

Stefano was behind the wheel. Enzo leaned out. "Let's get a move on it."

I recognized the focused gleam in both their eyes. The same urgency rode me. "I gave Tony one last shot."

"Mistake." Stefano's lips tightened, and he started the SUV.

Enzo gave a slight shake of his head. "Tony's good for hitting the clubs, but he doesn't have the intelligence for the darker side of this life. His methods don't yield the results they should. He doesn't read signs the way the rest of us do. He'll get an A for effort in backstabbing too. He takes after Antonio in the loyalty department." He pounded on the side of the door, my cue to move.

In the Mercedes, I led the way, and we flew out of the underground parking lot, through the city streets, then onto the highway that would take us to Antonio's residence.

As each mile evaporated to our target, my rage and helplessness grew. I firmly believed Tony didn't know where Antonio would take Liliana, which left Nicole. Somehow, we would get her to talk once we got the guards to give up her location.

We neared the long drive to Antonio's house. Soldiers were stationed at the gate. When they spotted us, they opened fire. I lowered my windows, the pings of bullets hitting the car as I returned fire. Stefano gunned the SUV, putting it between them and me. I ceased fire so as not to hit them, threw my car into park, and hopped out. Enzo's window was down, and he fired a machine gun at the guards. It was over almost as soon as it had started. All five men lay dead at the gate.

I ran to the guard box, pulled the slumped-over man out, then hit the button to open the gate. After I got into the back of the SUV, Stefano floored it, bumping over bodies as he sped to the front of the house. Enzo and I had guns out and firing as soon as we came to a stop.

The SUV was bulletproof. Eight guards were between us and the front door. "He didn't prepare!" I shouted over the noise. That told us he wasn't inside. "Would he protect Nicole?"

"Not likely," Stefano growled. "Stop, Enzo."

One guard was still standing. "We need answers." I hopped from the car, my gun aimed at his head. The guys also had him in their sights. If he shot me, they would drop in less than a second.

"Where's Antonio?"

"Not home." The soldier lowered his gun but didn't drop it.

"Liliana inside?"

He shook his head. "No. Antonio didn't bring her here."

I didn't think so. "Where's Nicole?" It was worth a shot.

"I don't know. She took one of the staff's cars late last night. That's all I know."

"Think carefully about your next moves." I backed up, getting into the SUV without a clue where Liliana was. Desperation was closing in, and I didn't know how long I could rein in the need for vengeance by annihilating everyone associated with Antonio.

CHAPTER TWENTY-SEVEN

LILIANA

Nicole laid down her cards, revealing a full house. "Read 'em and weep." When I tossed my two pairs on the cardboard box, she chuckled then added up our bottle cap pot and transferred what was in there into a total she maintained with the pencil stub she'd found in the same box as the discarded beer-top collection. She'd told me that was what they'd used when they played poker while she was growing up. Unfortunately, the bottle caps then had represented pennies to be paid later, which had been never been repaid. Ours were a hundred dollars per cap.

I rubbed my nose for probably the twentieth time. The dust was getting to me more than the headache that remained from whatever Antonio had shot into me.

My hands went to the small of my back, pushing on the sore muscles there, but that did nothing to ease the anxiety crawling through my mind over Max, and how I knew he wouldn't be able to find me. "Nicole, let's get out of here. I know you're doing what Antonio wants, but he'll forgive you if I get away, won't he?" I had no idea. Max would. For as driven and hard-core as I sensed him to be, I didn't fear harm from him no matter what I did.

"Oh, honey. You don't know Antonio that well. Remember that broken arm I had years ago?"

"Yes." I frowned. "You said you fell down the stairs." It had been believable because she drank a lot.

"That was from mouthing off to him and letting him know I didn't want to go to a function that he'd told me we were going to. He didn't yell at me. There was nothing to do to prepare for what he did." She shuddered. "He grabbed my arm and slammed it down on the edge of the dresser." She tossed back the rest of the contents in her glass. "When I realized how easy it was for him to do that to me, I never denied him anything again."

Her story brought back the night Mom was murdered and when Benito found us. I would never forget the look of devastation on his face at her death then his frightening transformation into a monster. While Antonio might have dished his punishments in silence to get his point across, Benito was the opposite. He'd shouted until he was hoarse, saying such horrible things that I didn't speak for a solid month after. Her death was my fault. He never wanted me. I was worthless. It went on and on. Then he'd hit me so hard that I flew across the closet and struck my head, cut it open, and promptly passed out. My fingers absently went to the crescent scar at my hairline above my temple.

"I'm sorry, Nicole. You shouldn't have to live like that." Gold digger or not, the sympathy I had for her own gilded cage grew tenfold. "What if I help you?"

"How would you propose to do that, honey? The guards won't let us leave." She splashed more amber liquid into her glass.

I held mine out for a refill. After she added another two shots, I took a small sip, set it down, then tucked my hair behind my ears. Holding her gaze, I let her see how serious I was about my proposal. "My guess is that Max will take over as boss. You already agreed that it's the most likely scenario. I have to wonder, though, will you seek revenge?"

She snorted. "That's not my way. I want the money I should get out of this marriage, never to have to work a day in my life, and to live in luxury." She sighed, and in that split second, the world-weary expression that settled over her made her look twenty years older. "I love my son, but he's made his choice, and one of them was to become just like his father. I'll be there for him, but not to help him hurt his half-brother. Honestly, I want out. I don't want to have to look over my back and wonder if someone will try to use me to get to my husband then pay the price by being a liability to Antonio." She lifted her glass in a mock salute. "His words."

I'd never seen Nicole like that before. It had to be because of our surroundings. "It wasn't too different, living under Benito's rule. I was never leaving that house unless he married me off to whoever benefited him the most." I clinked her glass with mine, building the camaraderie we had going. "With Benito, I was just as powerless. From what you've told me, having Tony was your ticket out of a life of poverty, but you didn't gain what you thought you would have. Antonio has mistresses?"

She bent her head down then lifted her drink. "You bet. I'm his trophy wife."

"I say we change that." I meant it too. Nicole might have been a little rough around the edges, but she was wicked smart and fun. Anxiety burned in my gut. Everything was riding on turning her to our side and helping Max to find us. "When Max takes Antonio out—we both know that's a very likely scenario— you'll be free. Why not get in his good graces and call him with our location?"

She pursed her lips, the gears turning as she tilted her head. "You're one smart cookie, sugar. And do I have your word in this arrangement as well? I will fall under both your and Max's protection, my fortune intact?"

"Do you have your phone?"

Nicole smirked then pulled a burner from her back pocket. "Never leave home without one."

"Call Max with our location and anything else you know, and we have a deal."

Max

The SUV ate up the miles between Antonio's clubs as we checked each one, leaving chaos in our wake. The sun crested the horizon, marking time since Lil was taken from me and put in harm's way. Tension was high in the vehicle. I wasn't the only one who wanted Liliana returned to us, unharmed.

"The dynamic between how the families run needs to change soon after we have Liliana." Stefano met my gaze in the rearview mirror. "We started this discussion before the commission. When she's back, we'll continue it."

I nodded in full agreement then scrubbed my face with my hand. I was going out of my mind. There hadn't been a single lead and no communication between Antonio and me. He'd gone dark. I needed a clue, even one, that would help me find her. When my phone vibrated in my pocket, a sliver of hope shone through the darkness of my thoughts.

I didn't recognize the number. Then Nicole's voice came through, and my heart stopped. "Hello, Max."

"Where is she?" I cut to all I cared about.

"Right here." There was some shuffling then she was back. "You're on speaker."

"Nicole," I growled, my patience nonexistent. I needed answers.

"I'm fine, Max. At least for now." The relief at hearing Liliana's sweet voice hit me like a Mack truck. "Nicole's been with me the entire time. She's helping me, and I've promised her our protection."

"Also from Antonio," Nicole cut in.

"What's stopping you from leaving?" I needed to know everything. How many men, their location, and where Antonio was in relation to them. I put the phone on speaker so Stefano and Enzo could hear about how to get to where they were.

"I don't know those details. But we're in the attic. Nicole will fill you in on the rest," Liliana said before Nicole took over.

"We're two hours from the city in a secluded two-story surrounded by forest." She rattled off the address, and Stefano screeched over and onto an off-ramp. "You'll need to hurry. Antonio will get here first. I'll try to hide us, but we can't leave the grounds. He has ten men watching the place. Two inside, the rest either in sight or not. I don't think there are more than that, but I can't be sure he told me the truth."

"We have a gun, a knife, and a Taser, but that's it," Lil added.

"Stay out of sight. Give us a chance to get to you." I glanced at the speedometer as we turned onto a ramp for another highway. We were going over ninety miles per hour and climbing.

"I'm sharing our location with you when I hang up." Nicole sounded hurried. "It'll make it easier to find us. This place is off the beaten path."

I didn't want to hang up, but they needed to hide. When Antonio got there, neither of them would be safe if Nicole had sided with Liliana.

"It could be an ambush," Enzo said as he reloaded the magazine in one of his Glocks.

"Doesn't matter."

"Oh, I'm not complaining." He turned in his seat, and I got a glimpse of the promise of death in his eyes. *Good. That's what I need from him today.*

Calls were made to Enzo's family, securing more men to help. We wouldn't need them, but it didn't hurt. The three of us were more than capable of taking down made men and even Antonio, should he arrive first. My gut churned. We had to beat him there.

We finished the drive in tense silence. We sped down narrow country roads, and my mind kept playing the same image over and over. Shooting Antonio in the head. I had no doubt that it would happen. A few hundred feet from where the house was, Stefano pulled off the road and into the forest. We got out and went in on foot.

The few clouds that were out provided relief from the morning sun. The canopy of branches overhead helped to diffuse some of the light. We moved quickly but with awareness. There could have been a sniper in one of the trees or lying behind a log.

Five feet out, we could see cars and the soldiers armed with machine guns, standing sentry around the dilapidated cottage.

A loud boom broke the silence and sent a flurry of birds lifting off from the surrounding trees. An ear-piercing scream sent cold dread slicing through me. And the gunshot that followed caused my heart to skip several beats. I took off in a run, firing on the soldiers as I went.

Return fire peppered the air around us. Stefano went left around the side of the house, Enzo right, and I barreled into the front door, crashing it open and against the wall. I put a bullet into the man inside, who dropped to the floor.

Movement in the room to the left made me whirl. The soldier's shot missed. Mine didn't.

"Max!"

Lil's scream alerted me to where she was. I pivoted as a thud sounded from the floor above. Then my body jerked back. I knew I'd been hit, but I felt nothing. When I tracked the source at the top of the landing, my world stopped.

Antonio stood there with Liliana, a shield in front of his body. A thin stream of blood ran from the side of her head. He had a knife at her throat, and a small trickle of blood trailed from where the tip had nicked her. Nicole was crumpled at his feet, unconscious or dead.

"Put down the gun," Antonio said with a growl.

"Don't do it." Lil whisper yelled.

"Shut up." Antonio tightened his hold on the knife against her delicate skin, and a thin red line appeared.

Fury flowed through my veins as I shifted the gun in my hand to the side, not ready to let go of it yet. Outside, the sounds of battle raged on, but it wouldn't last much longer.

"You won't get away with this. I have Tony. Think about what hurting Liliana will cost you." *Everything. It will cost him everything.* I knew he saw the promise of retribution in my eyes.

"I heard about the commission." His voice was smooth, controlled. "You've cost me too much already. You shouldn't have returned."

"I'll relinquish my claim if you let her go free." I would give anything for her. The threat to Liliana's life only made her worth that much clearer.

"Too late."

A shot pierced the window, slamming into Antonio's shoulder. His grip loosened on the knife. Lil pushed his arm. I brought my gun up as Nicole rolled over behind him, her arm arcing over her head. The knife in her hand sliced through Antonio's Achilles tendon. Lil shifted to the side, away from the edge of the knife. My fingers squeezed the trigger, sending a bullet into Antonio's chest as he listed to the side.

Racing toward the stairs, I rushed Liliana as her balance faltered. She was too close. Antonio could still harm her. He reached for her as I did. The distance was too great. I couldn't get to her. I couldn't let him take everything from me—which is what she was. I lunged forward.

Nicole rolled away as Antonio wobbled. His body crumpled against the rail. I took the stairs two at a time and caught Liliana as she fell. I yanked her to the side when a terrible crack sounded. The railing splintered. Twisting as we fell, I took the brunt of it. Air whooshed from my chest. Stunned, the world stilled. She was in my arms. *But is she safe?*

Antonio was on the ground, not far from us. *Alive.* Lil shifted, her eyes meeting mine. I sucked in a stilted breath, reveling in holding her safely in my arms.

Stefano strolled in and stood over us with a grin. "Graceful."

I grunted once I was able to take a full breath. It hadn't been that far of a drop. Still breathing, Antonio lay in a pool of expanding blood.

Nicole moaned from the top of the stairs, and Stefano left us to help her.

I didn't move right away because Lil was in my arms, and the feel of her eased the fear that had lived inside me since she'd been taken. She placed her hand over the wound at my shoulder.

"I wanted to kill him." Her voice shook with emotion.

"Your shouting saved my life." I brushed a few strands of her hair from her face to see where the blood was coming from. When she flinched, another wave of anger at Antonio surged. I dropped my hand, refusing to cause her more pain. This wasn't where we would stitch her up. Trey was waiting at our place. He would help.

Antonio shifted. Lil's eyes went wide, panic causing her pupils to expand in size. With a shove, I pushed Lil to my right. A gasp left her as she hit the floor, and I rolled to cover her body. My gun was clutched in my right hand and I shifted my arm to aim at Antonio.

He shot first, then I did. A small hole formed in his forehead from the bullet, red slowly filling it. Fury tore through me at where he'd aimed, and I fired several shots into his chest.

Cold stole through my veins. *Did the bullet go through my chest? Was she hit?*

Lil tugged at my shoulder, and a sense of overwhelming relief filled me. She was alive. I rolled to my back, skimming over every inch of her. There were no new wounds. I pulled her against my chest, my blood soaking into her clothes. But she didn't seem to mind.

I took in the red mark similar to a paper cut at her neck. It was minor, but it made me angry, and I wanted to shoot Antonio all over again. "Are you all right?" It came out in a growl as I worked to rein in my rage.

"Yes. Thank you for saving me again."

"All day, every day. But you should never have been in danger." We had a threat in Benito, and I wasn't sure about Frank Rossi's allegiance either. "Changes will be made."

She chuckled. "What do you have in mind?"

"There will be bodyguards assigned to you anytime you leave my presence. But what I want most of all is that you never leave my sight."

"Hmm. I could get on board with that."

I smoothed her hair from her face. "I love you, Liliana."

Tears filled her eyes, and that gorgeous smile I loved so much transformed her face to stunning. "I love you too."

"Let's get out of here."

She tried to scramble off me, but I held her tightly for another second before gaining our feet. Once outside, the five of us got in the SUV. Lil, Nicole, and I were in the back. Enzo and Stefano took the front, and Enzo made calls to alert his family of what they'd found and to relay that we were leaving. Then Trey was notified that we were on our way, so he could look over Lil and Nicole.

"I have to tell you something." Her eyes were sad, tears gathering there and threatening to spill down her cheeks. "Nicole told me that Benito killed your mom. Antonio knew."

I had suspected Benito was behind the accident but not that Antonio had figured it out and retaliated. "Antonio killed your mom, didn't he?"

When she nodded, I enveloped her in my arms. After a few minutes of comfort, she pulled away and gave me a closed-lipped smile. Our pasts were a mess, but it was time to put it behind us and build a stronger future.

With Antonio dead, Nicole was free—to an extent. She'd married into the Mafia, and a part of her would always be tied to us, but she would no longer live under Antonio's dominating rule.

On that note, I would be sworn in as the Caruso Mafia boss before the Sicilians returned home. I'd almost forgotten to tell her. "Your grandfather is here. He wants to see you, but I'm not willing to share you tonight." I nuzzled the side of her neck, whispering against her skin, "You were held at knifepoint in front of me. I need you. To feel you alive, healthy, and mine."

She shivered then shifted so her head lay on my chest, her arm around my waist. "I need the same."

I was never letting her go.

CHAPTER TWENTY-EIGHT

LILIANA

When we returned to our home, Sofia and Emiliana had rushed me, inspecting every cut and bruise. We'd clung to one another, and I'd shared everything. Max released Tony to Nicole after Trey looked her over. After that, he ushered everyone out. I understood. I needed to be alone with him too.

Max had fixed me something to eat for dinner after we'd showered—together. I loved the large space with the rainwater showerhead. Most of all, I loved the things Max had done to me in there.

We were in bed, sated and happy. With my legs tangled with his, my head rested on his chest as he ran his fingers through my hair. I could have fallen asleep in seconds if not for the constant pings from Max's phone.

Reluctantly, he picked it up and looked at the screen with a frown. "How the hell does everyone know where I live?"

I had to laugh. "Who is it?"

"Your grandfather." He let out a loud sigh. "We might as well get up. He won't go away. Stubborn old man."

We got up and dressed. Then he let my grandfather up. Nerves took flight in my stomach. I vaguely remembered meeting him on the few trips to Italy I'd taken with Mom when I was very young. But after she died, there had been no more contact, especially since Benito told me my grandfather had been the cause of my mom's death. Older and much wiser, I saw the lie for what it was—another way to control and isolate me.

Shaking the memories loose, I pasted a smile on my face as an older man with bushy white eyebrows and laugh lines stamped into his aging face came barreling off the elevator and into our living room. After he looked me over, he opened his arms. I went to him, enveloped in all the love I'd missed because of Benito. The scent of ocean and the floral hints of his favorite wine teased images from the past loose. Happy times with him and Mom surrounded me in familiarity.

He squeezed me tightly, and when he pulled back, holding me at arms' length, he called me Lily, and the dam broke. I fell back into his arms, memories of Mom and him surfacing and making me long for lost time.

"I've missed you, Lily." Tears pooled in Vincenzo's eyes.

We sat around the coffee table, and Max brought over wine. "I'm sorry. I should never have let Benito get in my head." All the time wasted broke my heart.

He patted my hand. "We have each other back now. We'll spend time in the vineyards when you come see me. You look so much like her."

I smiled, the compliment feeding that starved little girl who Benito tore down every chance he got. "Thank you. I miss her too."

"There will be plenty of time to reminisce about your mom when you come see me in Italy." He turned to Max. "Which will be soon?"

"Yes. We have to get a few things settled first. She has lots of family to meet."

Vincenzo laughed, the sound rich and throaty. I loved it instantly.

For the next several hours, the three of us got reacquainted, and Vincenzo made us promise again that we would come for a visit very soon. Max and I agreed and decided to take a honeymoon in Italy after he was sworn in as boss, which was to happen later that night at the swearing-in ceremony. A small amount of blood would be spilled from his finger onto Mario Caruso's saint card. Then Max would swear a sacred oath as the edge of the saint's card burned.

I couldn't have been happier. When Vincenzo left, I couldn't sit still and decided to confide in Max about what I wanted. There was something else I had to do, a confrontation long overdue.

The house I'd grown up in was dark where I stood by design. I hadn't been back there since Max forcibly removed me from the secret room. He wasn't far. It was something I had to do on my own, but after Antonio abducted me, Max couldn't deal with it. Still, I insisted he stay out of my way. The long overdue confrontation, I needed to have for myself.

I could hear Benito's voice as he moved through the house. Soon, he would enter the study, where he liked to have his brandy and cigars. The cloying scent clung to the heavy drapes and furniture. I hadn't spent any time in that room while growing up.

Benito wasn't alone. Max had his cousins doing surveillance outside, and through the earpiece that I wore, they gave an update about who Benito was with. Dino, his advisor, walked with him through the house. He couldn't be present while I confronted Benito, or the impact of what I had on him wouldn't be as weighty.

Benito was in the doorway, his portly body blocking the light, Dino behind him. He flicked the switch, and nothing happened. Then I turned on the lamp next to me. "Hello, Father."

With my head high and shoulders back, I gave him a minute to assess the situation. I didn't have a gun pointed at him. No one else was visible in the room. That alone would lower his guard. To him, I wasn't a threat. That, he had dead wrong.

Benito turned to Dino and told him they would talk in the morning. After a nod in my direction to acknowledge me, Dino left. I waited another minute until Benito came into the room. He moved to his armchair, flipped the lid on his cigar box open, removed one, and clipped the ends with a cigar cutter. With a flick of his thumb over a lighter, the orange flame illuminated his face. He extinguished it and puffed on the cigar a few times until the end was well lit.

I wasn't a fool. Even though he didn't have a gun pointed at me, he had the cutter, perfect for removing fingers, and a lit cigar he could burn me with. I wouldn't underestimate him, which was why I positioned myself where I had. There was a coffee table between us, and my back was to the north hallway. I could turn and outrun him or throw the knife that was strapped to my thigh, accessible through the slit of my long skirt.

It was time to get things going. I tilted my head to the side, scrutinizing him. Why I hadn't seen it before, I didn't know. "I always wondered why you hated me."

Benito froze. He stood by his chair, holding the cigar casually, but his cold eyes watched my every move. He had to have felt the crosshairs he was caught in, even if he didn't know exactly where I was going.

"You loved Mom. Worshipped her until that last year. But I'm getting ahead of myself." I offered a closed-lipped smile. "I have a few pictures of you that Mom had tucked away. You were very young in them. There were a few names on the back of the pictures of the same three people. One of them was Mom. That was easy. I recognized you too. But there was another boy, and he frequently had his arm around Mom. They looked happy, even in the one where she had her hand over her stomach while looking at him."

"What's the point to this? Whatever you think you know, you don't." His features remained impassive.

They wouldn't stay that way. I was prepared for the possibility of an epic explosion with the bomb I would drop. "From the look on her face and the position of her hand, it's obvious she was pregnant with me. The dates match. I did the math." I winked at him. "When I figured that out, everything made sense. The reason you didn't care about me was because I wasn't your child by blood."

"I raised you." He looked down his nose at me. "Gave you a roof over your head. You wanted for nothing."

"Not true." My voice rose. I took a steadying breath. Emotions would not aid me. Once calm, I continued. "As I said before, there were a few names to the pictures. One was a friend from town, Angelo Colombo. He had no family, no Mafia ties. The other, Benito, was a very distant cousin to the Rossi family. The one holding Mom wasn't you."

"You're wasting my time." He puffed on his cigar.

"Am I?" I tsked. "I don't think so. Another thing I found intriguing was how similar you and the other boy were. Same haircuts, similar frames. Although his shoulders were broader. Stronger jawline, maybe half an inch shorter. And his nose was a tad smaller." But he'd fixed the facial differences with plastic surgery, something Nicole had noticed.

He shifted as if to leave. I couldn't have that. I withdrew the picture I was talking about, a copy, from my pocket. "The man who's standing with mom is Benito Rossi. All I had to do was figure out who you are. Then I remembered something Mom said that last year. Getting her hooked on drugs didn't work in your favor. She liked to talk when she was high. Not at first, but when we were lying in the grass, watching the clouds shift overhead, she felt the freest, and her memories resurfaced in very interesting stories. At the time, I didn't know they were real. Now, I do."

"I don't know where you think you're going with this. You can't prove anything."

"You were Benito's friend. Mom said there was an accident. I'm curious. Was it an accident? That sort of thing seems to happen around you. Maria Caruso comes to mind."

"You shut your mouth before I shut it for you."

But he hadn't moved. Maybe he sensed Max was nearby. He would have been a fool not to. "Was it an opportunity for you to step into Benito's shoes, steal his girl, and assume his aspirations?"

His lips quirked, vying with the murderous expression in his dark gaze. "This is all speculation. You can't prove anything."

"But I can"—my voice came out whisper soft—"besides the pictures, and this is your copy." I tossed the replica on the table between us. "I have a letter from Mom, detailing everything that happened the day my real father died. How worried she was about what her father would say when he learned she was pregnant and how you stepped in, assuming Benito's life after you convinced her to flee to the United States with you. Promising that you would bring the Brambilla arm to America, joining the other families here to rule."

"Your mom was an addict. It's well known. Nothing she wrote matters. It's only the ramblings of a drug-induced haze."

"I have documents, blood tests, and a paternity test from when she sent your blood in after a time when you were wounded, along with mine. You're not my father. My blood type is O, the same as Mom. Yours is A and would have been dominant, but I don't have it. What do you think the chances are that my father's was also O?"

"We're done talking."

"For now. But know that if you ever come after me or Max

in any way, I'll ruin you. If something should happen, it will trigger the release of the detailed information we just discussed. Then, the families will come for you. I don't think they'll kill you right away, but you'll wish for it long before they put a bullet in your head."

I half turned to walk away when another thought occurred to me, and I paused. "You'll need to watch your back. I know you killed Max's mom. And he does too."

The cigar in Benito's hand broke in half, the lit end falling onto the rug below.

I lowered my voice to barely a whisper, sick with the knowledge of what Benito had done. "You were there the day his wife died, when his son was badly injured. The car they drove, you gave them the keys to it."

All color leached from Benito's ruddy cheeks.

"Antonio found out. Guess who had Mom killed?"

I left him there, the broken cigar smoldering on the rug. With two steps, I was in the dark hallway. Max emerged from the shadows and swept me to his side, his gun aimed at Benito, as it had been the entire time I was in the room with him.

"Are you all right?" His deep voice sent a shiver of awareness over my body.

"Yeah, I'm great." I grinned. For the first time in a very long time, a sense of power filled me. I had my life back. No one but me was in the driver's seat. As we moved through the house then exited through the rear entrance, I slipped my arm around his waist. Arranged marriage or not, marrying Max was the best decision I'd ever made. We were partners. I didn't lose anything by tying my life to his. I gained the world. "Let's go home."

His fingers tightened on me in response to my request, but he didn't drop his guard until we were clear of the house and at the car. Cristiano and Sal monitored our progress and would take out any threats that arose while we were in the open. I didn't think there would be any. I had Benito by the proverbial balls with his secret identity that would cause all the families to turn on him, rigged to a hair-trigger response system of information delivery if he harmed Max or me. It was a fantastic feeling to be free of the negativity and control he wielded.

As we neared the car, a figure appeared, leaning against the passenger side. Max had his gun pointed at him, but I stilled his arm, recognizing who it was as we got closer. "Dino." Benito's advisor, the only one who had been decent to me over the years.

"I never got a chance to congratulate you on the wedding." Then he turned to address me alone. "I helped Max with the contract, making sure Tony's name wasn't on there. Benito never noticed the last-minute swap. He was too focused on getting Antonio's signature on there."

"I…"—I had no words, no idea he'd been on our side—"thank you, Dino. Marrying Tony would—"

"Not even have been an option," Max cut in. "What are you going to do now?"

We would not let Dino's secret out, but there was danger in what he'd done, and anyone finding out would have cost him his life.

"My place is with the family. But my reason for seeking you out tonight is for one last gift. Your mother confided in me about many things, including the documents and pictures I know you have in your possession. There is something else you need to know about. You have a half-brother, Liliana, one who should be brought into the fold and eventually assume Benito's position as boss. Unless you want it?"

I wanted the freedom that vibrated around me more than anything. Taking over as the Brambilla boss wasn't something I had any desire to do. "No, I'm not interested in being boss." Not of that family. Of Max, absolutely. I shot him a mischievous wink, and he burst out laughing. *Message received.*

"I'll be in contact soon, Dino, and we can make plans to

locate Lil's half-brother and safely bring him into the fold without Benito's awareness."

Dino shook Max's hand then hugged me before blending into the shadows, out of sight of any of Benito's men.

"Let's go home." I rose onto my toes and brushed a kiss across his lips, pulling back before he could deepen the caress. I had plans for my husband when we got to our place—specifically, showing him who was boss.

CHAPTER TWENTY-NINE

MAX

Two weeks later...

A warm breeze whipped across the beach, sending a wide-brimmed hat cartwheeling through the white sand. We'd gone to Italy for ten days, five of which had already passed. I would never have enough time with her.

Everything around me, from the wisps of clouds in the blue skies and the cheery umbrellas a ways away from our private section of the beach to the rolling waves, could never have compared to the vision wading through the turquoise water—my wife—*heaven.*

Overheated from the sun, Liliana had gone to cool off while I finished a phone call to Sal, who had remained in Chicago to oversee things.

Before boarding the jet and as the new leader of the Caruso Italian-American family, I'd met with Vito, Antonio's advisor, to determine which of the businesses needed an overhaul. The vibe I'd gotten from him wasn't a good one. I'd set Sal up to work alongside him, monitoring and evaluating the day-to-day. Vito didn't know it, but Sal's business sense was spot-on, and he would take over as my second and advisor the day I returned. Changes would be made based on Sal's evaluation.

Lil and I had delivered on our word to Nicole. She'd suffered a minor concussion from Antonio clipping her with the butt of his gun. Back at the manor, she'd begun the process of overseeing the removal of Antonio's clothes and anything else she saw fit to donate or dispose of from the house.

As boss, I didn't want to live in my absentee father's home. That was for Nicole and Tony, should they wish to stay. Tony was a concern. While he'd gone through the motions when I was sworn in, even swearing fealty to the new boss, there was no mistaking the hatred that burned in his eyes. Relieved of his position as second, I'd put men I could trust in place to monitor him.

Retaliation would happen, but I would be ready for it.

That worry was for another day. The present was for Lil. She and I were discussing plans to build a house, and ground would break once they were finalized. We were close to a decision, and I looked forward to sharing the home we designed together.

Everything in me stilled as she emerged from the frothing waves, a virtual goddess. Tossing my phone to the towel, I got to my feet. A smile curved her lips. Then she read my intent, and her eyes heated with passion too.

"Is our beach day over?" she purred.

Water beaded on her flawless golden skin, shimmering like diamonds as the sun worked to dry them. The purple hue in her blue eyes was even more brilliant with the backdrop of the ocean. Then my gaze dropped to her bee-stung lips, and all I could think about was my need to taste them. The teal string bikini she wore was driving me crazy. My hand settled on her hip, the other along the delicate curve of her neck.

Her pupils dilated, and a soft gasp left her parted lips, my invitation to take. As I tugged her to me, her soft, sun-warmed skin met mine. I bent my head as she tilted her face then took her lips in a kiss that had her moaning for more and me struggling to control myself.

I would never let her go.

With reluctance, I ended the kiss. Taking her hand in mine, I led her in the direction of our towels then bent to toss my phone into the beach bag containing our guns. We'd come back for the rest later or the next day. It didn't matter. That part of the beach was private, all ours.

The bag was over my shoulder, and I released her hand and wrapped my arm around her waist to pull her closer. The wind teased a long strand of her blond hair loose from the messy bun she wore. Side by side, we crossed the beach to climb the long flight of tiered stairs that led to our home on the hill.

I'd purchased it a few years before because I'd fallen in love with the tourist-free coastal town. The views were spectacular from the house, and I'd bought the surrounding lots for added privacy. It had been a retreat for me alone but had become a sanctuary for Lil and me to come to whenever we could get away. If possible, I would have stayed there with her, letting the world we lived in take a back seat. But I had an empire to run when we returned and a vendetta to settle with Benito.

A phone rang in our bag, and Lil laughed, the sound light, airy. "No rest for the wicked."

I grinned. "I'll show you wicked right here and now if you don't pick up the pace."

Liliana

W e raced up the remaining steps, laughter trailing us as we burst through the screen door to our oceanfront villa. Ceiling fans swirled in a slow paddle above as we crossed the lanai to the door that led to our bedroom. I felt a tug at my back as my bikini top loosened. I lifted it from my neck as Max pulled the rest of my suit down. It tangled around my legs, and I listed, about to fall. I shrieked as his arms went around me. He then lifted me against his warm, bare chest.

My laughter died at his hungry expression, and I shivered at the promise in his eyes. My body responded—softening, swelling, preparing. I wanted him, then and always.

My hand trailed along the taut muscles of his shoulders to cup the back of his neck, drawing him closer, needing to feel his lips on mine.

He laid me on our bed then followed. I welcomed his weight as he settled over me, heat radiating from his larger body. Then he took my lips in a toe-curling kiss. I buried my fingers in his hair, and when he broke the kiss, I tugged gently. He complied by trailing kisses along my neck. His teeth scraped along the sensitive pulse-point at the curve where my shoulder met my neck, and I moaned at the delicious pressure that spiraled through my body from what he was doing.

Releasing the strands of his hair that I'd gripped, my fingers traced the muscles that flexed in his back until rounding to his abdomen then lower. Taking his hard length in my hand, I gently squeezed. The guttural moan rumbling through his chest sent a heady surge of power through me. It didn't last. He took control again, tugging my arm away. He caressed my thigh then lifted my leg so that it wrapped around his waist. My body heated, my breath coming faster as I squirmed against the hard length of him, desperate to increase the friction.

My head spun. Desire built to uncontrollable heights. He played my body like a fine-tuned instrument with each caress and kiss until I was arching beneath him, digging my nails into his shoulders, urging him on.

"Max, please," I begged him to fill me, shaking with need.

His dilated gray eyes met mine, passion turning them obsidian as his guttural voice sent another wave of desire through me. "I'll never get enough of you, Lil."

I arched against him as he pressed against my core. When he filled me, I cried out at the rightness of us. His muscles flexed and bulged as he moved over me with each powerful thrust. I dug my nails into his back, urging him to go faster. Then he claimed my mouth in an intoxicating kiss as I neared a climax. When his fingers dipped between us, caressing my sensitive bundle of nerves, my head rocked back against the pillow, and I cried out. Cresting waves burst behind my eyelids, and my body convulsed around him, urging him to follow. His movements quickened, then he chased my climax with his own.

We stayed connected as our heart rates regulated. In his arms, I felt well-loved. Content. Relaxed in the protection of his embrace.

When he pulled out, I felt the loss instantly. He drew me close as he shifted to the side. The connection we shared was more than I'd ever dreamed I could have. It was worth fighting for. I was never letting him go.

Max

I shifted to the side so as not to crush Lil but continued to hold her close. As if wanting to maintain the connection as much as I did, she tangled her legs with mine, her palm resting over my heart. I brushed a few strands of hair from her cheek, adding them to the mass spread across the pillow.

The windows were open, and the rhythmic back-and-forth

of the waves filtered through to my awareness. It was easy to get lost in Lil, letting everything else go. And in Italy, we were able to let our guard down more than we could in the States.

My heart swelled as the love I had for her soared through me. There wasn't anything I wouldn't do for her.

I couldn't help but remember the first time I'd seen her, wanting to share just how much she meant to me. "I fell in love with the idea of you from a picture Vincenzo gave me."

She grinned. "That must have been some picture."

She had no idea. "When we met, you were so much more than I'd imagined."

"I remember seeing you get out of your car that first day at Benito's house. You had a presence that drew me to you. So strong and confident." Her fingers trailed down my chest. "All this rippling muscle. I knew in that moment I was in deep trouble, that there would be no coming back from you." Her teeth caught her bottom lip, drawing my focus from her expressive eyes. "This is where I'm meant to be. With you."

Lil snuggled closer, her gaze softening and pulling me in like she always did.

The first time we laid eyes on one another was burned into my psyche, too, and I cherished and guarded it. "In that one moment, you became my world."

I had one final thought in the seconds before I lost myself in her. I would forever be grateful for the love my mother's relatives had shown me. They had helped to fill the majority of the hole in my heart—my soul—left by my father. But even their love hadn't been enough to close it. Lil's was.

"I love you, Max." She tugged on the back of my neck, drawing me to her for a kiss I was helpless to resist. "You're my world too."

The End

Continue reading the Mafia Elite series with Blood Oath.
https://www.amazon.com/gp/product/B098LY9WBB/
https://amymckinleyauthor.com/mafia-elite/

BLOOD OATH

Tragedy brought them together, and tragedy tore them apart.

Heir to a throne, Chicago Mafia underboss Enzo Vitale will do anything to keep Sofia safe, but his presence in her life puts a target on her back. He must protect the love of his life at all costs, even if it means staying away from her—a goal that runs against every fiber of his being.

Up-and-coming fashion designer Sofia La Rosa fell in love with her best friend years ago. She'll sacrifice anything for Enzo, even as a wall of secrets steadily builds between them.

But secrets don't stay hidden forever. When the enemy learns of Sofia's involvement in a former cover-up, they're out for blood, driving her to the very man who vowed to be her savior no matter the cost.

Click the link to order!
https://www.amazon.com/gp/product/B098LY9WBB/
https://amymckinleyauthor.com/mafia-elite/

If you enjoyed reading NO WAY OUT as much as I did writing it, I hope you'll consider leaving a review.

ACKNOWLEDGMENTS

This will be short and sweet! Several people who are there for me each step of the way from start to finish, and I am beyond grateful for their support and encouragement. Huge thank you to my husband and four kids, who are amazing. I'm truly lucky.

I have an incredible team of editors. Taylor Anhalt always has a significant role in the development of my books. I loved her content edit and how she helped to shape this story into what it is today. I have a fabulous team from Red Adept Editing. Kate Birdsall has been editing for me for the past two years, and I'm so lucky to be working with her. She helps to make my stories better and gets my thought process. Working with her is so much fun.

My critique partners, Kristin Kisska, Emily Albright, and Candace Irvin, who are amazing authors themselves, are always willing to jump into every book, and I value their creative input. I'm thankful to have them in my inner circle.

T.E. Black Designs, who did the cover design, is a dream to work with. No matter the genre, she understands my vision and can match that with the genre's vibe. As always, each project exceeds my expectations.

I'm grateful to have Danielle Sanchez with Wildfire Marketing Solutions and Colleen Noyes with Itsy Bitsy Book Bits in my corner working their magic to make each release a success.

Last but certainly not least, a special thank you to all the bloggers and readers who have encouraged and helped me along the way and who continue to make my dream a reality.

Thank you.

ABOUT THE AUTHOR

 Amy McKinley is the *USA Today* bestselling author of the romantic suspense thriller Gray Ghost Novels, Deadly Isles Special Ops, Covert Recruits, Mafia Elite, Moonlit Destination Series, the Five Fates paranormal romance books, and several standalone titles. Her edge-of-your-seat books are filled with surprising twists and just the right amount of heat and danger. She lives in Illinois with her husband, two daughters, two sons, and three mischievous cats.

You can find her at:
www.AmyMcKinley.com

Subscribe to Amy's newsletter for cover reveals, book announcements, and giveaways:
http://eepurl.com/dEBqJn

facebook.com/amymckinleyauthor
bookbub.com/authors/amy-mckinley
instagram.com/amymckinleyauthor
twitter.com/AmyMcKinley7

ALSO BY AMY MCKINLEY

Gray Ghost Novels

Moments That Define Us

Broken Circle

Eye of the Storm

Beneath the Surface

Vantage Point

Covert Threat

Marked for Death

Deadly Isles Special Ops

Twisted Secrets

Bound by Secrets

Forged by Secrets

Mafia Elite

No Way Out

Blood Oath

Born in Darkness

Bloodlines

Covert Recruits (coming soon)

Irina

Sasha

Zena

Nadia

Katya

Standalone Titles

Shattered Melody

Siren's Call: Cursed Seas

Fake Fiancé (A Second Chance Office Romance)

Moonlit Destination Series

Moonlit Whisper

Moonlit Kiss

Moonlit Mirage

Five Fates Series

Hidden

Taken